ALSO BY HAN KANG

The Vegetarian

Human Acts

A NOVEL

Han Kang

TRANSLATED FROM THE KOREAN AND INTRODUCED BY

DEBORAH SMITH

HOGARTH

LONDON/NEW YORK

Published in the United States by Hogarth, an imprint of the Crown
Publishing Group, a division of Penguin Random House LLC, New York.
crownpublishing.com

HOGARTH is a trademark of the Random House Group Limited, and
the H colophon is a trademark of Penguin Random House LLC.

This book was originally published in Korean as 소년이 온다
("The Boy Is Coming"), in 2014 by Changbi Publishers, Inc.
Copyright © 2014 by Han Kang. This translation originally published, in
slightly different form, in Great Britain by Portobello Books, London.
This edition published by arrangement with Portobello Books.

Library of Congress Cataloging-in-Publication Data
Names: Han, Kang, 1970– author. | Smith, Deborah, 1987– translator.
Title: Human acts : a novel / Han Kang ; translated from the Korean and
introduced by Deborah Smith.
Other titles: Sonyæon i onda. English
Description: First U.S. edition. | New York : Hogarth, 2016.
Identifiers: LCCN 2016002979
Subjects: LCSH: Democratization—Korea (South)—History—20th
century—Fiction. | Korea (South)—Politics and government—1960—
Fiction. | Political fiction.
Classification: LCC PL992.26.K36 S6613 2016 | DDC 895.73/5—dc23 LC
record available at http://lccn.loc.gov/2016002979

ISBN 978-1-101-90672-9
Ebook ISBN 978-1-101-90673-6
International Edition 978-1-5247-6017-5

Printed in the United States of America

Book design by Lauren Dong
Jacket design by Michael Morris
Jacket photographs: (rib cage) Sebastian Kaulitzki/Shutterstock; (magpie) Dethan
Punalur/Getty Images; (leaves) Sam Scott-Hunter/Getty Images

10 9 8 7 6 5 4 3 2 1

First U.S. Edition

Human Acts

INTRODUCTION

In early 1980, South Korea was a heap of dry tinder waiting for a spark. Only a few months previously Park Chung-hee, the military strongman who'd ruled since his coup in 1961, had been assassinated by the director of his own security services. Presiding over the so-called Miracle on the Han River—South Korea's rapid transformation from dirt-poor and war-shattered into a fully industrialized economic powerhouse—had gained Park support from some quarters, though numerous human rights abuses meant he was never truly popular. Recently, he'd succumbed to the classic authoritarian temptation to institute increasingly repressive measures, including scrapping the old constitution and having a new one drawn up making his rule a de facto dictatorship. By 1979 things were fraying at the edges, and Park's declaration of martial law in response to demonstrations in the far south was, to some, a sign that something had to give.

But the assassination was no victory for democracy. Instead, into Park's place stepped his protégé Chun Doo-hwan, another army general with firm ideas on how a people should be governed. By May Chun had used the excuse of rumored North Korean infiltration to expand martial law to the entire country, closing universities, banning political activities, and further curtailing the freedom of the press. After almost two decades of Park Chung-hee, South Korean citizens recognized a dictator when they saw one. In the southern city of Gwangju, student demonstrations had their numbers swelled by those for whom the country's "miraculous" industrialization had meant backbreaking work in hazardous conditions, and for whom recent unionization had led to greater political awareness. Paratroopers were sent in to take over from the police, but their brutality against unarmed citizens resulted in a still greater turnout in support of the civil militias. Together, they managed a brief respite during which the army retreated from the city center.

Shoot-outs, heroism, David and Goliath—this is the Gwangju Uprising as it has already been told in countless films, and a lesser writer might have been tempted to start with such superficially gripping tropes. Han Kang starts with bodies. Piled up, reeking, unclaimed, and thus unburied, they present both a logistical and an ontological dilemma. The alternation in the original between words whose meanings shade from "corpse" or "dead body" to "dead person" or simply "body" reflects a status of uncertainty reminiscent of *Antigone*. In the Korean context, such issues can also be connected to animist beliefs and the idea of somatic integrity—that violence done to the body is a violation of the spirit/soul that animates it. In Gwangju, part of the magnitude of the crime was that the violence done to these bodies, and the manner in which they had been dumped or hidden away, meant they were unable to be identified and given the proper burial rites by their families.

The novel is equally unusual in delving into the complex background of the democratization movement, though Han Kang's style is always to do this obliquely, through the experiences of her characters, rather than presenting a dry historical account. There is the class element, much of which floats beneath the surface of the novel; because the recently unionized factory girls were some of the most vocal and visible agitators for change, the authorities were able to paint the uprising as a Communist plot sparked by North Korean spies, thus legitimizing their brutal crackdown. In the chapter entitled "The Prisoner, 1990," I paid special attention to diction in the hope that this would highlight the subtle politics of a working-class torture survivor being pressured into revisiting traumatic memories for the sake of a university professor's academic thesis. And there is also gender politics, with "The Factory Girl, 2002," featuring a women-only splinter group from the main union, set up to address the fact that female workers were treated more unfairly even than the men.

Another striking feature of the uprising is regionalism. It was no accident that the first rumblings, and the worst violence, were felt in the far south of the Korean peninsula, a region that has a long history of political dissent, and of underrepresentation in the central government. It also goes some way in explaining why the uprisings were suppressed with such brutality, and why the government was able to cover up the precise details and statistics of this suppression for so long. It wasn't until 1997 that the massacre was officially memorialized, and casualty figures remain a contentious issue even today. Disputing the official figures was initially punishable by arrest and, despite being far lower than the estimates by foreign press, these have still not been revised. In terms of mentality if not geography, Gwangju was sufficiently far from Seoul to seem "off the mainland"—the same kind of mental distance as that from London to Northern Ireland at the time of the Bloody Sunday massacre.

Born and raised in Gwangju, Han Kang's personal connection to the subject matter meant that putting this novel together was always going to be an extremely fraught and painful process. She is a writer who takes things deeply to heart, and was anxious that the translation maintain the moral ambivalence of the original, and avoid sensationalizing the sorrow and shame that her hometown was made to bear. Her empathy comes through most strongly in "The Boy's Mother, 2010," written in a brick-thick Gwangju dialect impossible to replicate in English, Korean dialects being mainly marked by grammatical differences rather than individual words. To me, "faithfulness" in translation primarily concerns the effect on the reader rather than being an issue of syntax, and so I tried to aim for a nonspecific colloquialism that would carry the warmth Han intended. Though I did smuggle in the tiniest bit of Yorkshire—call it translator's license.

One of this translation's working titles was *Uprisings*. As well as the obvious connection to the Gwangju Uprising itself, a thread of words runs through the novel—*come out, come forward, emerge, surface, rise up*—which suggests an uprising of another kind. The past, like the bodies of the dead, hasn't stayed buried. Repressed trauma erupts in the form of memory, one of the main Korean words for "to remember" meaning literally "to rise to the surface"—an inadvertent, often hazy recollection that is the type of memory most common in Han Kang's book. Here, chronology is a complex weave, with constant slippages between past and present, giving the sense of the former constantly intruding on or shadowing the latter. Paragraph breaks and subheadings have been inserted into the translation in order to maintain these shifts in tense without confusing the reader.

In 2013, when Park Chung-hee's daughter Park Geun-hye was inaugurated as president, the past rose up and ripped the bandage off old wounds for Gwangju-ites like Han Kang. Her novel, then, is both a personal and political response to these recent developments, and a reminder of the human acts of which we are all capable, the brutal and the tender, the base and the sublime.

Deborah Smith

1

The Boy, 1980

L ooks like rain," you mutter to yourself.
    What'll we do if it really chucks it down?
    You open your eyes so that only a slender chink of light seeps in, and peer at the gingko trees in front of the Provincial Office. As though there, between those branches, the wind is about to take on visible form. As though the raindrops suspended in the air, held breath before the plunge, are on the cusp of trembling down, glittering like jewels.

When you open your eyes properly, the trees' outlines dim and blur. You're going to need glasses before long. This thought gets briefly disturbed by the whooping and applause that breaks out from the direction of the fountain. Perhaps your sight's as bad now as it's going to get, and you'll be able to get away without glasses after all?

"Listen to me if you know what's good for you: come back home, right this minute."

You shake your head, trying to rid yourself of the memory, the anger lacing your brother's voice. From the speakers in front of the fountain comes the clear, crisp voice of the young woman holding the microphone. You can't see the fountain from where

you're sitting, on the steps leading up to the municipal gymnasium. You'd have to go around to the right of the building if you
wanted to have even a distant view of the memorial service. Instead, you resolve to stay where you are, and simply listen.

"Brothers and sisters, our loved ones are being brought here
today from the Red Cross hospital."

The woman then leads the crowd gathered in the square in a
chorus of the national anthem. Her voice is soon lost in the multitude, thousands of voices piling up on top of one another, a soar-
ing tower of sound rearing up into the sky. The melody surges to a
peak, only to swing down again like a pendulum. The low murmur
of your own voice is barely audible.

This morning, when you asked how many dead were being
transferred from the Red Cross hospital today, Jin-su's reply was
no more elaborate than it needed to be: thirty. While the leaden
mass of the anthem's refrain rises and falls, rises and falls, thirty
coffins will be lifted down from the truck, one by one. They will
be placed in a row next to the twenty-eight that you and Jin-su
laid out this morning, the line stretching all the way from the
gym to the fountain. Before yesterday evening, twenty-six of
the eighty-three coffins hadn't yet been brought out for a group
memorial service; yesterday evening this number had grown to
twenty-eight, when two families had appeared and each identified
a corpse. These were then placed in coffins, with a necessarily
hasty and improvised version of the usual rites. After making a
note of their names and coffin numbers in your ledger, you added
"group memorial service" in parentheses; Jin-su had asked you to
make a clear record of which coffins had already gone through the
service, to prevent the same ones being brought out twice. You'd

wanted to go and watch, just this one time, but he told you to stay at the gym.

"Someone might come looking for a relative while the service is going on. We need someone manning the doors."

The others you've been working with, all of them older than you, have gone to the service. Black ribbons pinned to the left-hand side of their chests, the bereaved who have kept vigil for several nights in front of the coffins now follow them in a slow, stiff procession, moving like scarecrows stuffed with sand or rags. Eun-sook had been hanging back, and when you told her, "It's okay, go with them," her laughter revealed a snaggle-tooth. Whenever an awkward situation forced a nervous laugh from her, that tooth couldn't help but make her look somewhat mischievous.

"I'll just watch the beginning, then, and come right back."

Left on your own, you sit down on the steps that lead up to the gym, resting the ledger, an improvised thing whose cover is a piece of black strawboard bent down the middle, on your knee. The chill from the concrete steps leaches through your thin track-suit bottoms. Your PE jacket is buttoned up to the top, and you keep your arms firmly folded across your chest.

Hibiscus and three thousand ri full of splendid mountains
    and rivers . . .

You stop singing along with the anthem. That phrase "splendid mountains and rivers" makes you think of the second character in "splendid," "*ryeo*," one of the ones you studied in your Chinese script lessons. It's got an unusually high stroke count; you doubt you could remember how to write it now. Does it mean "mountains and rivers where the flowers are splendid," or "mountains and rivers that are splendid as flowers"? In your mind, the image of the written character becomes overlaid with that of hollyhocks, the kind that grow in your parents' yard, shooting up taller than you in summer. Long, stiff stems, their blossoms unfurling like little scraps of white cloth. You close your eyes to help you picture them more clearly. When you let your eyelids part just the tiniest fraction, the gingko trees in front of the Provincial Office are shaking in the wind. So far, not a single drop of rain has fallen.

The anthem is over, but there seems to be some delay with the coffins. Perhaps there are just too many. The sound of wailing sobs is faintly audible amid the general commotion. The woman holding the microphone suggests they all sing *"Arirang"* while they wait for the coffins to be got ready.

You who abandoned me here
Your feet will pain you before you've gone even ten ri . . .

When the song subsides, the woman says, "Let us now hold a minute's silence for the deceased." The hubbub of a crowd of thousands dies down as instantaneously as if someone had pressed a mute button, and the silence it leaves in its wake seems shockingly stark. You get to your feet to observe the minute's silence, then walk up the steps to the main doors, one half of which has been left open. You get your surgical mask out from your trouser pocket and put it on.

These candles are no use at all.

You step into the gym hall, fighting down the wave of nausea that hits you with the stench. It's the middle of the day, but the dim interior is more like evening's dusky half-light. The coffins that have already been through the memorial service have been grouped neatly near the door, while at the foot of the large window, each covered with a white cloth, lie the bodies of thirty-two people for whom no relatives have yet arrived to put them in their coffins. Next to each of their heads, a candle wedged into an empty drinks bottle flickers quietly.

You walk farther into the auditorium, toward the row of seven corpses that have been laid out to one side. Whereas the others have their cloths pulled up only to their throats, almost as though they are sleeping, these are all fully covered. Their faces are revealed only occasionally, when someone comes looking for a young girl or a baby. The sight of them is too cruel to be inflicted otherwise.

Even among these, there are differing degrees of horror, the worst being the corpse in the very farthest corner. When you first saw her, she was still recognizably a smallish woman in her late teens or early twenties; now, her decomposing body has bloated to the size of a grown man. Every time you pull back the cloth for someone who has come to find a daughter or younger sister, the sheer rate of decomposition stuns you. Stab wounds slash down from her forehead to her left eye, her cheekbone to her jaw, her left breast to her armpit, gaping gashes where the raw flesh shows through. The right side of her skull has completely caved in, seemingly the work of a club, and the meat of her brain is visible. These open wounds were the first to rot, followed by the many bruises on her battered corpse. Her toes, with their clear pedicure, were initially intact, with no external injuries, but as time passed they swelled up like thick tubers of ginger, turning black in the process. The pleated skirt with its pattern of water droplets, which used to come down to her shins, doesn't even cover her swollen knees now.

You come back to the table by the door to get some new candles from the box, then return to the body in the corner. You light the cloth wicks of the new candle from the melted stub guttering by the corpse. Once the flame catches, you blow out the dying candle and remove it from the glass bottle, then insert the new one in its place, careful not to burn yourself.

Your fingers clutching the still-warm candle stub, you bend down. Fighting the putrid stink, you look deep into the heart of the new flame. Its translucent edges flicker in constant motion, supposedly burning up the smell of death that hangs like a pall in the room. There's something bewitching about the bright orange glow at its heart, its heat evident to the eye. Narrowing your gaze even further, you center in on the tiny blue-tinged core that clasps the wick, its trembling shape recalling that of a heart, or perhaps an apple seed.

You straighten up, unable to stand the smell any longer. Looking around the dim interior, you drag your gaze lingeringly past each candle as it wavers by the side of a corpse, the pupils of quiet eyes.

Suddenly it occurs to you to wonder, when the body dies, what happens to the soul? How long does it linger by the side of its former home?

You give the room a thorough once-over, making sure there are no other candles that need to be changed, and walk toward the door.

When a living person looks at a dead person, mightn't the person's soul also be there by its body's side, looking down at its own face?

Just before you step outside, you turn and look back over your shoulder. There are no souls here. There are only silenced corpses, and that horrific putrid stink.

At first, the bodies had been housed not in the gymnasium, but in the corridor of the complaints department in the Provincial Office. There were two women, both a few years older than you, one wearing a wide-collared school uniform and the other in ordinary clothes. You stared blankly, forgetting for a moment why you'd come, as they wiped the bloodied faces with a damp cloth and struggled to straighten the stiff arms, to force them down by the corpses' sides.

"Can I help you?" the woman in school uniform asked, pulling her mask down below her mouth as she turned to face you. Her round eyes were her best feature, though ever-so-slightly protruding, and her hair was divided into two braids, from which a mass of short, frizzy hairs were escaping. Damp with sweat, her hair was plastered to her forehead and temples.

"I'm looking for a friend," you said, holding out the hand that you'd been using to cover your nose, unused to the stench of blood.

"Did you arrange to meet here?"

"No, he's one of those . . ."

"I see. You can come and have a look, if you like."

You systematically examined the faces and bodies of the twenty-odd people lying against the corridor wall. You had to look closely if you wanted to be sure; your eyes soon started to feel the strain, and you had to keep blinking to try and refocus.

"Not here?" the other woman asked, straightening up. She had the sleeves of her pale green shirt rolled up to the elbows. You'd assumed she was a similar age to the young woman in school uniform; seeing her without the mask on, though, you could see she was older, more like twenty. Her skin was somewhat sallow, and she had a slender, delicate neck. Only the look in her eyes was tough and vigorous. And there was nothing feeble about her voice.

"No."

"Have you tried the mortuary at Jeonnam, and the one at the Red Cross hospital?"

"Yes."

"What about this friend's parents?"

"His mother passed away, and his father works in Daejeon; he lives in our annex with his older sister."

"They still won't put long-distance calls through?"

"No, and I've tried a few times."

"Well, what about your friend's sister?"

"She hasn't been home since Sunday; I came here to look for her, too. One of our neighbors said they saw my friend get hit yesterday, when the soldiers were shooting."

"Mightn't he just have been wounded and admitted to hospital?" the woman in school uniform interjected, without looking up.

You shook your head.

"In that case he would have found a way to call us. He'd know we were worrying about him."

"Come by again tomorrow, and the next couple of days," said the woman in the pale green shirt. "Apparently all the dead will be brought here from now on. They say there's no room left in the morgues."

The woman in school uniform wiped the face of a young man whose throat had been sliced open by a bayonet, his red uvula poking out. She brushed the palm of her hand down over his staring eyes, closing them, rinsed the cloth in a bucket of water, and wrung it out viciously. The water that came out was dark with blood, splattering outside the bucket. The woman in the green shirt stood up.

"How about you give us a hand, if you have time?" she asked. "Just for today. We don't have enough people. It's not difficult . . . you just need to cut up that cloth over there and use it to cover the bodies. And when someone comes looking for a friend, like you did, you uncover them again. The faces are badly injured, so they'll need to get a good look at their bodies and clothes to decide whether it's who they think it is."

From that day on, you became one of the team. Eun-sook, as you'd guessed, was in her final year of high school. Seon-ju, the woman in the green shirt, was a machinist at a dressmaker's on the main shopping street; she'd been left in the lurch when the boss had decided that he and his son, who'd been studying at one of the universities here, should go and stay with a relative outside the city. Both Eun-sook and Seon-ju had gone to give blood at Jeonnam University Hospital after hearing a street broadcast saying that people were dying of blood loss. There, hearing that the Provincial Office, now being run by civilians, was short of hands, and in the confusion of the moment, they'd taken on the task of dealing with the corpses.

In the classroom, where seats were assigned in order of height, you were always the one at the very front—in other words, the shortest. Since March, when you'd started your third year at middle school, you'd finally hit puberty, resulting in a slightly lower voice and a fair-to-middling growth spurt, but you still looked younger than your age. Jin-su's work mostly kept him confined to the briefing room; the first time he saw you, he looked surprised.

"You're a first-year, aren't you? This is no place for you." Jin-su's deeply lidded eyes and long lashes were almost feminine; the university in Seoul he was attending was temporarily closed, so he'd come down to Gwangju.

"No," you told him, "I'm a third-year. And I don't have a problem with the work here."

This wasn't bravado; there was nothing technically difficult about the tasks you'd been assigned. Seon-ju and Eun-sook had already done most of the heavy work, which involved covering plywood or Styrofoam boards with plastic, then lifting the corpses on top of these boards. They also washed the necks and faces with a cloth, ran a comb through the matted hair to tidy it a bit, then wrapped the bodies in plastic in an effort to combat the smell. In the meantime, you made a note in your ledger of gender, approximate age, what clothes they were wearing and what brand of shoes, and assigned each corpse a number. You then wrote the same number on a scrap of paper, pinned it to the corpse's chest, and covered them up to the neck with one of the white cloths. Eun-sook and Seon-ju would then help you pull them over to the wall. Jin-su, who seemed to be permanently rushed off his feet, would come striding up to you several times a day, wanting to transfer the information you'd recorded in your ledger onto posters, to put up at the main entrance to the building. A lot of the people who came looking for someone had either seen those posters themselves or been told about them by someone else. In cases of a positive identification, you would retreat to a respectful distance to wait for the sobbing and wailing to pass. As the corpses had been given only a cursory treatment, it was left to the bereaved to stop their noses and ears with cotton wool and give them a fresh change of clothing. Once they had been thus simply dressed and placed into a coffin, it was your job to oversee the transfer to the gym, and make a note of everything in your ledger.

The one stage in the process that you couldn't quite get your head around was the singing of the national anthem, which took place at a brief, informal memorial service for the bereaved families, after their dead had been formally placed in the coffins. It was also strange to see the Taegukgi, the national flag, being spread over each coffin and tied tightly in place. Why would you sing the national anthem for people who'd been killed by soldiers? Why cover the coffin with the Taegukgi? As though it wasn't the nation itself that had murdered them.

When you cautiously voiced these thoughts, Eun-sook's round eyes grew even larger.

"But the generals are rebels, they seized power unlawfully. You must have seen it: people being beaten and stabbed in broad daylight, and even shot. The ordinary soldiers were following the orders of their superiors. How can you call them the nation?"

You found this confusing, as though it had answered an entirely different question to the one you'd wanted to ask. That afternoon there was a rush of positive identifications, and there ended up being several different shrouding ceremonies going on at the same time, at various places along the corridor. The national anthem rang out like a circular refrain, one verse clashing with another against the constant background of weeping, and you listened with bated breath to the subtle dissonance this created. As though this, finally, might help you understand what the nation really was.

• • •

The next morning, you and the two women carried several of the most putrid bodies out to the yard behind the Provincial Office. So many new bodies were arriving, there was no more space to lay them out inside. Jin-su came marching from the briefing room, brisk as always, and demanded to know what you were planning to do if it rained.

He frowned as he scanned the passageway, where the corpses had their feet jammed up against the wall. Seon-ju unhooked her mask.

"It's too narrow here," she said, "there's just no way. There'll probably be more corpses arriving in the evening, so what'll we do then? How about the municipal gym? Isn't there space there?"

Four men showed up less than an hour later, sent by Jin-su. They must have been standing guard somewhere, as they had rifles slung over their shoulders and were wearing visored helmets, which the riot police had left behind. While they loaded the bodies into a truck, you and the two women packed up the sundries. You followed the truck over to the gym, walking slowly in the balmy morning sunlight. Passing beneath the still-adolescent gingko trees, you reached up mechanically to tug at the branches, the lowest of which brushed against your forehead.

Eun-sook led the way, and was first to enter the gym. When you went inside, you saw that she'd been brought up short by the sight of the coffins filling the hall. The cotton gloves she was clutching were dappled with dark bloodstains. Seon-ju, who'd been bringing up the rear, stepped around you and tied up her shoulder-length hair with a handkerchief.

"I didn't realize they'd been bringing them all here . . . seeing them all together like this, my God, there's so many."

You looked around at the bereaved, who were kneeling practically back-to-back. Each family had stood a framed portrait photograph on the coffin they were watching over. Some coffins also had a pair of glass Fanta bottles standing side by side at their head. One of the bottles held a bunch of white flowers, and the other, a candle.

That evening, when you asked Jin-su if he could get hold of a box of candles, he nodded eagerly.

"Of course, candles, that'll get rid of the smell."

Whenever you told Jin-su there was something you needed—whether it be cotton cloth, wooden coffins, scrap paper, flags—he would jot it down in his notebook and within the same day, seemingly out of nowhere, it would materialize. He told Seon-ju that every morning he went to either Daein or Yangdong Market, and if there was something that couldn't be got there, he went and hunted it down in woodworking shops, funeral parlors, drapers, all across the city. There was still a lot of money left over from the donations that had been collected at the meetings, and when he said he was representing the Provincial Office, many people chose to give him a hefty discount on whatever it was he wanted, sometimes waiving the fee altogether. Money, then, wasn't the issue. But now the city had run out of coffins, so he'd got hold of as much plywood as they thought they'd need and a new batch was currently being assembled at the carpenters'.

The morning Jin-su arrived with five boxes of fifty candles each, and matchboxes, you scoured every nook and cranny of the building, collecting any drinks bottles you spotted that could be used to hold the candles. The bereaved queued at the table by the entrance while you lit each candle and inserted it into one of the bottles. They then carried the bottle over to their coffin and set it down at the head. There was more than enough to go around. Enough even for the still-unidentified corpses, and those coffins that had no one to watch over them.

Every morning new coffins were brought to the gym, where a group memorial altar had been set up. The new arrivals were those who had breathed their last while undergoing treatment at the hospital. When the bereaved families brought in the coffins, pushing them in handcarts—was it sweat or tears that made their faces shine?—you had to move the existing coffins closer together to make room.

In the evenings, people were brought in who had been shot in the suburbs, in confrontations with the army. They had either died instantly, from the soldiers' gunfire, or while being taken to hospital. Many of them hadn't been dead long and still looked uncannily alive; Eun-sook would be trying to stuff a jumble of spilled, opaque intestines back inside a gaping stomach when she'd have to stop what she was doing and run out of the auditorium to throw up. Seon-ju, frequently plagued by nosebleeds, could often be seen with her head tipped back, pressing her mask over her nose.

Compared with what the two women were dealing with, your own work was hardly taxing. Just as you had at the Provincial Office, you recorded date, time, clothing, and physical characteristics in your ledger. The cloths had already been cut to the appropriate size, and each scrap of paper had been attached to a clothes peg, ready to be pinned straight to the corpse once the number had been written on it. As the need arose for new places, you pushed the still-unidentified closer together, followed by the coffins. On nights when the influx of new arrivals was especially overwhelming there was neither the time nor the floor space to neatly rearrange the existing order, so the coffins just had to be shoved together any old way, edge to edge. That night, looking around at all those dead bodies crammed into the gym hall, you thought to yourself how much like a convention it seemed, a mass rally of corpses who were all there by prearrangement, whose only action was the production of that horrible putrid smell. You moved swiftly among this silent congregation, clasping your ledger under your arm.

It really is going to chuck it down, you think, drawing in a deep breath as you emerge from the dim, twilit world of the gymnasium. You head for the backyard, wanting to drink in more of that clean air, but stop at the corner of the building, worried about straying too far from your post. Now the voice coming from the speakers is that of a young man.

"We cannot just hand in our weapons and surrender unconditionally. First they have to return our dead to us. They also have to release the hundreds they've thrown in prison. And more than that, we have to make them promise to admit the true facts about what happened here, so we can recover our honor in the eyes of the rest of the country. After that, there wouldn't be any reason for us not to return their firearms, would there? What do you all say?"

You sense that the cheers and applause that follow are coming from a much smaller number of people than before. You remember the assembly that was convened the day after the soldiers withdrew. Then, there were so many people that the overflow crowded onto the roof of the Provincial Office and the clock tower. The streets were laid out like a paduk board, with no vehicles permitted entry, and what had been the only available space had been taken up by the buildings. A great mass of people, more than a hundred thousand strong, surged through those streets with the rippling motion of colossal waves. Their voices joined together for the national anthem, the swelling chorus rising up like a tower, a story for every voice. The sound of their clapping was like thousands of fireworks being let off in succession. Yesterday morning, you listened to Jin-su and Seon-ju discussing what was going to happen. Looking serious, Jin-su had said that there was a rumor going around that when the soldiers came back, those who were gathering in the streets would all be killed, and so the demonstration was being hastily scaled down. "We need there to be more of us, not less, if we're to prevent the army from reentering the city . . . the mood's not good. Every day there are more coffins; people are starting to think twice about venturing out of doors."

"Hasn't enough blood been shed? How can all that blood be simply covered up? The souls of the departed are watching us. Their eyes are wide open."

The voice of the man conducting the ceremony cracks at the end. The repetition of that word, "blood," gives you a tightening feeling in your chest, so you open your mouth wide and suck in another deep breath.

A soul doesn't have a body, so how can it be watching us?

You recall your maternal grandmother's death last winter.

What started out as a mild cold soon turned into pneumonia, and she was admitted to the hospital. She'd been there around a fortnight when you and your mother went to visit her, one Saturday afternoon when you were basking in the relief of having got through the end-of-term exams. But then, without warning, your grandmother's condition deteriorated. Your mother contacted her brother and told him to come as quickly as possible, but he was still stuck in traffic when the old woman breathed her last.

Your childhood visits to her home inevitably included a quiet "follow me" as the elderly woman, her back bent into the shape of the letter ㄱ, led the way to the dark room that was used as a pantry. Then, you knew, she would open the larder door and bring out the cakes that were stored there to use as ceremonial offerings on the anniversary of a relative's death: pastries made from oil and honey, and block-shaped cakes of pounded glutinous rice. You would take an oil-and-honey pastry with a conspiratorial grin, and your grandmother would smile back at you, her eyes creasing into slits. Her death was every bit as quiet and understated as she herself had been. Something seemed to flutter up from her face, like a bird escaping from her shuttered eyes above the oxygen mask. You stood there gaping at her wrinkled face, suddenly that of a corpse, and wondered where that fluttering, winged thing had disappeared to.

What about those who are now in the gym hall—have their souls also escaped their bodies, flying away like birds? Where could they possibly be going? It surely wasn't some alien place like heaven or hell, which you'd heard about the one time you ever went to Sunday school, when you and your friends were lured there by the prospect of chocolate Easter eggs. You'd never been convinced by the historical dramas on TV, where the spirits of the dead were supposed to be scary figures, dressed all in white and wandering around in an eerie fog, their disheveled hair the sign of an unquiet rest.

You feel drops of rain pattering down on your head. As you look up, the raindrops splash against your cheeks and forehead. Seemingly in an instant, the individual drops meld and blur into thick streaks, pouring down with ferocious speed.

The man with the microphone shouts out, "Please sit down, all of you. The memorial service hasn't finished yet. This rain is tears shed by the souls of the departed."

The chilly rainwater, which has crept inside the collar of your uniform, soaks your vest as it trickles down your back. *The tears of souls are cold, all right.* Goose bumps rise on your forearms, on your back, as you hurry to shelter under the eaves projecting over the main door. The trees in front of the Provincial Office are being lashed by the rain. Squatting down on the highest step, the one closest to the door, you think back to your biology lessons. Studying the respiration of plants during fifth period, when the sunlight was always on the wane, seems like something that took place in another world, now. Trees, you were told, survive on a single breath per day. When the sun rises, they drink in a long, luxurious draft of its rays, and when it sets, they exhale a great stream of carbon dioxide. Those trees over there, who hold those long breaths within themselves with such unwavering patience, are bending under the onslaught of the rain.

Had that other world continued, you would have sat your midterms last week. Today being Sunday, and with no more exams to prepare for, you would have slept in late before going out to play badminton in the yard with Jeong-dae. The time of that other world seems no more real, now, than does the past week.

It happened last Sunday, when you'd gone out alone to buy some practice papers from the bookshop in front of the school. Frightened by the sight of armed soldiers, who seemed to have materialized out of nowhere, you took a side alley leading down to the riverside. A couple were walking opposite you, the man wearing a suit and holding a Bible and hymn book, and the woman in a navy-blue dress. Something about the way they were talking made you think they must be newlyweds. A thin scream rang out several times from the top of the road, and three soldiers carrying guns and clubs raced down over the hilltop, surrounding the young couple. They looked to have been pursuing someone, and to have turned down this alley by mistake.

"What's the matter? We're just on our way to church . . ."

Before the man in the suit had finished speaking, you saw a person's arm—what? Something you wouldn't have thought it capable of. Too much to process—what you saw happen to that hand, that back, that leg. A human being. "Help me!" the man shouted, his voice ragged. They kept on clubbing him until his twitching feet finally grew still. The woman stood there and screamed when she should have just backed off; you saw them grab her by the hair, but you don't know what happened after that. You were too busy crawling, trembling, into the next street, a street where a sight even further from your experience was unfolding.

You jerk your head up in alarm, startled witless by the hand that just brushed your right shoulder. A slender, outstretched hand that seems wound around with cold scraps of cotton, like some fragile apparition.

"Dong-ho."

Eun-sook, soaked to the skin from her braids to the hems of her jeans, bends down over you and laughs.

Your face white as a sheet, you muster a halfhearted chuckle in response. *You dummy, what would a ghost need hands for?*

"I meant to come back earlier; sorry you got caught up in this rain. . . . I was worried that if I left, the others would start leaving, too. Has anything much happened?"

You shake your head. "No one came looking for anyone. No passersby either."

"It was the same at the service. Not many people came."

Eun-sook squats down next to you and pulls a sponge cake out of the pocket of her hoodie, the wrapper rustling. A yogurt pot follows it.

"The church aunties were handing these out, so I thought I might as well get some."

You hadn't even realized you were hungry; now you tear off the plastic wrapper and cram the sponge cake into your mouth. Eun-sook peels the lid off the yogurt and hands it to you.

"I'll stay here for now; you can go home and change. If anyone was going to come, they would have been and gone by now."

"No, you go, I barely got wet," you say, mumbling around a mouthful of sponge cake. You swallow the cake and gulp down the yogurt.

"The Provincial Office doesn't exactly have many home comforts, you know," Eun-sook says delicately. "And it's hard work you've been doing . . ."

You blush; you know you stink of sweat. Whenever you go to wash your hands in the tiny annex bathroom, you always try to give your hair a quick wash, too. The putrid smell seems to have soaked into your skin, so at night you even splash the cold water over your whole body, teeth chattering and sneezing violently; now it seems you might as well not have bothered.

"I heard at the assembly that the army is coming back into the city tonight. If you go home, stay there. Don't try and come back tonight."

Eun-sook draws up her shoulders, and the hairs escaping from her braids tickle the nape of her neck. You watch in silence as her fingers smooth her wet hair and pluck at her sweater. Her face, which had had a chubby cuteness to it when you first saw her, has grown gaunt in the space of a few days. You fix on her eyes, which have become hollow and shadowed, and think, *whereabouts in the body is that bird when the person is still alive? In that furrowed brow, above the halolike crown of that head, in some chamber of the heart?*

You cram the last of the cake into your mouth and pretend you hadn't heard what Eun-sook just said about the army.

"What's a bit of sweat?" you say. "It's people who've got drenched from the rain who ought to go and change."

Eun-sook fishes another yogurt out of her pocket.

"This was supposed to be for Seon-ju. . . . Take your time with this one, don't just wolf it down. No one's going to snatch it out of your mouth!"

You accept it greedily, peel back the lid with your fingernail, and grin.

Seon-ju, unlike Eun-sook, isn't the kind to creep up on you unde-tected and quietly put a hand on your shoulder. As she walks over, she's still several meters away when she calls your name in her clear, strong voice.

"No one came?" she asks, as soon as she's near enough not to have to shout. "You've just been here on your own?" She plonks herself down on the steps next to you and thrusts a roll of foil-wrapped *gimbap* in your general direction. You pinch a piece between your fingers and pop it into your mouth while Seon-ju stares out at the gradually lessening rain.

"So you still haven't found your friend?" The question is blurted out without any preamble, and you need a moment before shaking your head in reply. "Well," Seon-ju continues briskly, "seeing as you've not had any luck so far, the soldiers have probably buried him somewhere." You rub your chest; the dry chunk of seaweed-wrapped rice seems suddenly difficult to get down. "I was there too, you see. That day. The soldiers picked up those who got shot close to them and loaded them into a truck." Anticipating the words that might rush out next, you jump in.

"You're soaked," you say. "You should go home and change. Eun-sook's gone already."

"What for? Once we start work again this evening, we'll be sweating buckets." Seon-ju folds and refolds the empty aluminum foil until it's down to the size of a little finger, gripping it in her fist as she watches the rain coming down. Her profile makes her look composed and resolute, and a question bubbles up inside you.

Will those who stay behind today really all be killed?

You hesitate, and think better of voicing these thoughts. *If it looks like that's what's going to happen, surely they should all clear out of the Provincial Office and go and hide at home. How come some leave and others stay behind?*

Seon-ju flicks the scrap of foil in the direction of the flower bed, examines her empty hand, then scrubs vigorously at her tired-looking eyes, her cheeks, her forehead, even her ears.

"I can't keep my eyes open. Maybe I'll just nip to the annex . . . find a comfy spot on one of the sofas and snatch a quick nap. I can dry my clothes while I'm at it." Seon-ju laughs, revealing her compact front teeth. "I'm leaving you all alone again, poor old Dong-ho!"

Perhaps Seon-ju is right; perhaps the soldiers took away Jeong-dae and buried him somewhere. On the other hand, though, your mother's still convinced that he's being treated at some hospital, that the only reason he hasn't been in touch is that he's still not regained consciousness. She came here with your middle brother yesterday afternoon, to persuade you to come home. When you insisted that you couldn't go home until you'd found Jeong-dae, she said, "It's the ICU you ought to be checking. Let's go around the hospitals together."

She clutched the sleeve of your uniform.

"Don't you know how shocked I was when people said they'd seen you here? Good grief, all these corpses; aren't you scared?"

"The soldiers are the scary ones," you said with a half-smile. "What's frightening about the dead?"

Your middle brother blanched. Your brother, the straight-A student who'd spent his childhood studying as though nothing else existed, only to make mistake after mistake in the university entrance exams. He was currently on his third try. He took after your father with his broad face and thick beard, making him look much older than his nineteen years. By contrast, your eldest brother, a ninth-grade civil servant in Seoul, is much more delicately built—you could almost call him pretty. When he comes back down to Gwangju during the holidays and the three of you are together, it's your middle brother whom everyone mistakes as the eldest.

"Paratroopers from the Special Warfare Command, with their tanks and machine guns—you really think they're quaking in their boots at the thought of a bunch of civilians who only have clapped-out rifles that haven't been fired since the war? You think that's why they haven't reentered the city? They're just biding their time and waiting for orders from higher up. If you're here when they return, you'll be killed."

You take a step back, worried he's going to give you a clip around the ear.

"What reason do they have to kill me?" you say. "I'm just lending a hand with a couple of things, that's all." You wrench his arms away and shake free of your mother's clinging hands. "Don't worry, I'll just finish helping out and then I'll come home. After I've found Jeong-dae."

You run inside the gymnasium, waving awkwardly over your shoulder.

The sky, which has been gradually clearing, is dazzlingly bright all of a sudden. You stand up and walk around to the right-hand side of the building. The square is practically empty now that the crowd has dispersed. There are only the bereaved left, mono-chrome figures clustered near the fountain in groups of two and three. The bereaved, and a handful of men transferring the coffins from beneath the rostrum onto a truck. Squinting, trying to make out individual faces, your eyelids tremor in the face of this harsh smack of light. Minute spasms travel down to the muscles in your cheeks.

There wasn't a scrap of truth in what you told Eun-sook and Seon-ju, that first day at the Provincial Office.

In that same square you're looking at now, where hordes of people gathered to demonstrate, from old-timers in their fedoras to boys of twelve and women carrying colorful parasols, that day when they loaded the corpses of two men who had been shot in front of the train station into a handcart and pushed it at the very head of the column, it wasn't a neighbor who caught that last glimpse of Jeong-dae, it was you yourself. And it wasn't as though you just caught sight of him from a distance; you were close enough to see the bullet slam into his side. At first the two of you were hand in hand, excitedly making your way to the front. Then the ear-splitting sound of gunfire tore through the afternoon and everyone was pushing and shoving, trying to run back the way they'd come. Someone shouted, "It's okay, it's just blanks!" One group tried to push back to the front again, and Jeong-dae's hand slipped from yours in the turmoil. Another deafening cannonade of shots, and Jeong-dae toppled over onto his side. You took to your heels and fled. You pressed yourself up against the wall of an electrical goods store, next to the lowered shutter. There were three older men there with you. Another man, who seemed to be part of their group, was running over to join them when a spray of blood suddenly erupted from his shoulder and he fell flat on his face.

"Good God, they're on the roof," the man next to you muttered. "They shot Yeon-gyu from the roof."

Another burst of gunfire rang out from the roof of the next

building along. The man Yeon-gyu, who had been staggering to his feet, flipped backward as though someone had pushed him over. The blood spreading from his stomach washed greedily over his chest. You looked up at the faces of the men standing next to you. No one said anything. The man who'd spoken was shaking silently, his hand over his mouth.

You opened your eyes a fraction and saw dozens of people lying in the middle of the street. You thought you saw a pair of light blue tracksuit bottoms, identical to the ones you were wearing. Bare feet—what had happened to his sneakers?—seemed to be twitching. You tensed, about to dash over, when the man standing next to you seized hold of your shoulder. Just then, three young men ran out from the next alleyway along. When they shoved their hands under the armpits of the fallen and hauled them up, a burst of rapid-fire gunshot exploded from the direction of the soldiers in the center of the square. The young men crumpled like puppets whose strings had been cut. You looked over at the wide alley adjoining the opposite side of the street. Thirty-odd men and women were pressed up against the wall, a frozen tableau, their staring eyes riveted to the scene in front of them.

A few minutes after the gunfire had ceased, a strikingly diminutive figure dashed out, unhesitating. The man ran as fast as he could toward one of the people lying on the ground. When another burst of rapid-fire gunshot put paid to his efforts, the man who'd been keeping a firm grip on your shoulder moved his large, coarse hand to cover your eyes, saying, "You'll only be throwing your life away if you go out there now."

The moment he took his hand away, you saw two men from the opposite alleyway run toward a young woman as though pulled by a huge magnet, grab her arms, and lift her up. This time the gunfire rang out from the roof. The men somersaulted head over heels.

After that, there were no more rescue attempts.

Around ten minutes of tense silence had passed when a couple of dozen soldiers stepped out of their column, walking in pairs toward those who had fallen nearest them. They worked swiftly and methodically, dragging them back to the other soldiers. As though this were the cue they'd been waiting for, a dozen men ran out from the next and opposite alleyway, to lift up those who had fallen farther back. This time, no shots rang out. The men who'd been standing with you left the safety of the wall to retrieve a group who had breathed their last, then hurriedly disappeared down the alleyway. And yet, you made no move to go and help Jeong-dae. Left alone, you were frightened and, thinking only about avoiding the snipers' sharp eyes, shuffled quickly sideways along the wall, your face pressed up against the bricks, your back turned to the square.

The house was quiet that afternoon. Despite all the upheavals, your mother had still gone to open up your family's leather shop in Daein Market, and your father, who'd injured his back a while ago carrying a heavy box of hides, was lying down in the inner room. You pushed open the main gate, which was always left with one half unlocked, the metal rasping against the stone. As you stepped into the yard, you heard your middle brother chanting English vocabulary in his room.

"Dong-ho?" Your father's voice carried clearly from the main room. "Is that Dong-ho come back?" You didn't answer. "Dong-ho, if that's you, then get in here and give my back a trample."

Giving no sign of having heard, you walked across the flower bed and pushed down on the handle of the pump. Cold, clear water crackled into the nickel washbasin. You plunged your hands in first, then scooped up the water to splash over your face. When you tilted your head back the water ran down over your jaw, along the line of your throat.

"Dong-ho, that is you outside, isn't it? Come in here." With your dripping hands pressed against your eyes, you remained standing on the stone terrace. After a while, you slipped your feet out of your sneakers, stepped up onto the wooden veranda, and slid open the door of the main room. Your father was lying prone in the center of the room, which was thick with the smell of moxa cautery.

"The muscle was giving me pain earlier, and I couldn't get up. Give it a trample down near the base."

You peeled off your socks and lifted your right foot up onto your father's lower back, careful not to press down with your full weight.

"Where've you been gadding off to? Your mother kept phoning to ask if you'd got back. It's not even safe to go around the neighborhood, with this demo. Last night there was shooting over by the station, and some people were even killed . . . it doesn't bear thinking about. How can anyone go up against a gun with nothing but an empty fist?"

You switched feet with a practiced movement and cautiously pressed down between your father's spine and sacrum. "Ah, that's the spot, just there . . ."

You left the inner room and went into your own, next to the kitchen. You curled up into a fetal position on the papered floor. Sleep sucked you down so suddenly it was like losing consciousness, but not many minutes had passed before you started awake, jolted out of a terrifying dream whose details were already impossible to remember. In any case, the waking hours that stretched out in front of you were far more frightening than any dream. Naturally, there were no sounds of anyone moving around in the room Jeong-dae shared with his sister, a tiny annex off the main gate. Nor would there be when evening came. The light would stay switched off. The key would stay skulking at the bottom of the dark brown glazed jar next to the stone terrace, undisturbed.

Lying in the hush of the room, you see Jeong-dae's face with your mind's eye. You see those pale blue tracksuit bottoms thrashing, and your breathing becomes constricted, as though a ball of fire has lodged itself in your solar plexus. Struggling for breath, you try to replace this image with that of Jeong-dae on a perfectly ordinary day, or right now, pushing open the main gate and stepping into the courtyard as though nothing had happened. Jeong-dae, who still hadn't had the growth spurt that usually comes in middle school. Whose older sister, Jeong-mi, found a way to get milk for him even when times were tight, hoping it would make him grow. Jeong-dae, whose plain features made you marvel that he could be related to Jeong-mi. Who still managed a certain appeal in spite of his flat nose and buttonhole eyes, who could bring about general hilarity just by screwing up his nose and deploying his megawatt grin. Whose disco dancing at the school talent show, his cheeks blown out like a puffer fish, had made even the scary form teacher burst out laughing. Who was more interested in making money than in studying. Whose sister nevertheless gave him no choice but to prepare for the entrance exams for liberal arts college. Whose paper route was carried out behind the back of this same sister, the bitter evening wind whipping his cheeks red as soon as winter set in. Who had an ugly wart on the back of his hand. Who, when you played badminton together in the yard, was incapable of playing any shot other than a smash, seemingly under the illusion that he was representing the South Korean team in some international match.

Jeong-dae, who nonchalantly slid the blackboard cleaner into his book bag.

"What're you taking that for?"

"To give to my sister."

"What's she going to do with it?"

"Well, she keeps talking about it. It's her main memory of middle school."

"A blackboard cleaner? Must have been a pretty boring time."

"No, it's just there was a story connected with it. It was April Fool's Day, and the kids in her class covered the entire blackboard with writing, for a prank—you know, because the teacher would have to spend ages getting it all off before he could start the lesson. But when he came in and saw it he just yelled, 'Who's classroom monitor this week?'—and it was my sister. The rest of the class carried on with the lesson while she stood out in the corridor, dangling the cloth out of the window and beating it with a stick to bash the chalk dust out. It is funny, though, isn't it? Two years at middle school, and that's what she remembers most."

You slowly pushed yourself up, palms braced against the cold paper floor. Walked to the door, slid it open, put your slippers on. Shuffled across the narrow courtyard and stopped in front of the annex. You reached down into the glazed jar, thrusting your arm in all the way up to your shoulder, and rummaged around. The key clanked and scraped against the earthenware; your fingers closed around it, and you fished it out from underneath the mallet and hammer. The lock on the annex door clicked open. You slid off your slippers and stepped inside.

The room showed no signs of recent disturbance. The notebook was still lying open on the desk, just as you remembered it from Sunday night, when Jeong-dae had been close to tears and you'd thought to calm him down by making a list of places Jeong-mi might have gone to. Evening classes; the factory; the church she occasionally attended; her uncle once removed in Ilgok-dong. The next morning, the two of you had called in at all those places, but Jeong-mi was nowhere to be found.

You stood in the center of the room, the day darkening around you, and rubbed your dry eyes with the backs of your hands. You kept on rubbing until the flesh was hot and tender. You tried sitting at Jeong-dae's desk, then lay prone with your face pressed to the chilly floor. You ground your fist into the concavity at the center of your sternum, which was starting to throb. If Jeong-mi were to come in through the main gate right this second, you would race over and fall to your knees at her feet, beg her to go with you to look for Jeong-dae among the bodies lined up in front of the Provincial Office. *Isn't he your friend? Aren't you a human being?* That's what Jeong-mi would scream while she thrashed you. And you would beg her forgiveness while she did.

Just like her brother, Jeong-mi is small for her age. On top of that, her short bob means that from the back, she looks like a senior student at middle or even primary school, though she's actually just turned nineteen. From the front, too, she can easily pass for a high-school first-year, though she attempts to look a little older by always wearing makeup. Despite her feet being swollen from standing up all day, she insists on wearing high-heeled shoes for the walk to and from work. Far from being the type to thrash anyone, her light tread and quiet voice make it impossible to imagine her ever getting properly angry. And yet, according to Jeong-dae, she had strong opinions on certain matters, and was more than capable of holding her own in a debate. *It's just that people don't know. She's actually even more stubborn than my dad.*

In the two years she and Jeong-dae have been living in your annex, you've never once had a proper conversation with Jeong-mi. She worked at a textile factory, and was frequently on night shifts. Jeong-dae, too, was often home late—because of his paper route, though to his sister he pretended to have been studying at the library—so the coal fire in the annex kept going out that first winter. On evenings when she got home before her brother, you'd hear her soft knock on your door. Face haggard with exhaustion, short hair tucked behind her ears, *excuse me, the fire . . .* it seemed an effort for her just to part her lips. Every time that happened you would spring to your feet and hurry over to the fireplace, pick out some hot briquettes with the tongs, and hand them to Jeong-mi in a long-handled pan. *Thank you,* she would say, *I didn't know what to do.*

The first time the two of you exchanged more than this handful of words was one early winter's evening the previous year. Jeong-dae had tossed his book bag into a corner as soon as he got home from school, then headed straight back out for his paper route. He still wasn't back when you heard what to you was the unmistakable sound of her knock. So tentative, as though she was afraid of harming the wood, as though the tips of her fingers had been swaddled in soft rags. You opened the door straightaway, and stepped out into the kitchen.

"I was just wondering, I don't suppose you still have any of your first-year textbooks?"

"First-year?" you echoed dully, and she explained that she was planning to attend night school starting from December.

"The world's changed since they assassinated President Park. The labor movement's gathering strength, and now our bosses can't force us to work overtime anymore. They're saying our salaries will go up, too. This could be a great opportunity for me, I need to take advantage of it. I want to start studying again. But I've been out of school so long, I'm not sure I'd be able to just pick up where I left off; I want to go back over the things we did in the first year before I make a go at anything else . . . then, by the time Jeong-dae's on holiday, I should be okay to move on to the second-year stuff."

You asked her to wait just a moment, then clambered up into the loft. Her eyes widened when you climbed back down, bearing an armload of dusty textbooks and reference books.

"My goodness . . . what a steady young man you are, holding on to all this stuff. Our Jeong-dae threw all his out as soon as he was done with them." She accepted the books, adding, "Please don't tell Jeong-dae about this. He knows it was because of him that I couldn't keep on with my studies, and he already feels bad enough as it is. So please don't let the cat out of the bag until I've passed the high-school entrance exams."

You stood there staring at her smiling face, dumbfounded by this unprecedented volubility, and by the blossoming in her bright eyes, pale petals unfurling from tightly closed buds.

"Perhaps, once Jeong-dae's gone on to university, I might even be able to follow in his footsteps. University. It's possible, if I study hard enough. Who knows?"

At the time, you doubted whether she would be able to keep her studies a secret. If Jeong-dae came home to find her with those textbooks spread open, where in their tiny single room could she possibly hide them? Behind her skinny back? And Jeong-dae usually stayed up late to do his homework, so it wasn't as though she could just wait until he'd fallen asleep.

After only a brief while, these doubts were replaced by more intimate imaginings. The soft fingers that would peel open the pages of your textbook, mere inches from Jeong-dae's sleeping head. The soft upward curve of those lips as they repeat: *My goodness, what a steady young man he is, holding on to all this stuff* . . . those affable eyes. That exhausted smile. That muffled-sounding knock. You felt lacerated by everything you imagined going on in the annex, a bare couple of yards from the room where you spent the nights tossing and turning. In the early hours of the morning, when you heard her stepping out into the courtyard and washing her face at the pump, you would bundle yourself up in the quilt and crawl over to the door, pressing your ear against the paper, your eyes, heavy with sleep, still closed.

The second truckload of coffins pulls to a stop in front of the gym. Squinting even more than usual because of the sun's flat glare, you manage to pick out the figure of Jin-su, climbing down from the front passenger seat. His brisk steps carry him in your direction.

"We're closing the doors here at six. Make sure you've gone home by then."

"Who will look after the—the people inside?" you stammer.

"The soldiers are reentering the city tonight. Even the bereaved will be sent home. There mustn't be anyone still here after six."

"But why would the soldiers bother coming here? What harm could the dead possibly do them?"

"According to them, even the wounded lying in hospital beds are a 'mob' that need finishing off. Does it really seem likely that they'll just turn a blind eye to all these corpses, to the families watching over them?"

Jin-su bites down on whatever else he was going to say, and marches past you into the gymnasium. You presume that he's about to say the very same thing to the bereaved. Clutching the ledger to your chest as you would a treasured possession, you stare after his retreating figure, at the sense of responsibility stiffening his shoulders. You squint to make out Jin-su's wet hair, wet shirt, wet jeans, the profiles of the bereaved as they either shake or nod their heads. A woman's quavering voice becomes increasingly shrill.

"I'm not going to budge an inch. I'll die here, at my baby's side."

You turn your gaze to the people lying farthest inside the hall, with cloths pulled right up over their heads; those who still haven't had anyone come and identify them. You force yourself to focus on the person in the corner. The moment you first set eyes on her, in the corridor of the Provincial Office, you thought, *Jeong-mi*. Though the face hadn't yet begun to putrefy, the deep knife wounds that marked it made the features difficult to discern. But it seemed similar, somehow. And that pleated skirt. Yes, it was definitely similar.

But that kind of skirt's quite common, isn't it? Are you really sure you saw her go out in a skirt like that on Sunday? Was her hair really as short as that? That bob looks like it belongs to a proper middle-schooler, doesn't it? And why would Jeong-mi, constantly having to scrimp and save to make ends meet, have been so extravagant as to get a pedicure when it wasn't even summer? But you never did get a good look at her bare feet. Only Jeong-dae would know if Jeong-mi had that dark-blue splotch on her knee, barely the size of a red bean. You need Jeong-dae to be able to know, categorically, that the woman lying there is not his sister.

On the other hand, though, you need Jeong-mi to help you find her brother. If she was here in your place, she would have gone around every hospital in the city, until she came across her brother in one of the recovery rooms, just that minute coming to his senses. Like when he'd rushed out of the house last February, insisting to Jeong-mi that he'd die before he went to liberal arts school, that as soon as he got to the middle of third year he was going to start taking the vocational classes that would be offered then, to prepare you for the world of business. With an almost uncanny swiftness she'd tracked him down in some comics store that very same day and dragged him out by the ear. Your mother and middle brother had found the sight of Jeong-dae being hauled around by such a petite, unassuming young woman utterly hilarious. Even your father, a dour and taciturn man, found it difficult to keep from laughing, and had to clear his throat loudly several times. The two siblings retreated to their annex, and their muffled exchange could be heard going on until after midnight. When one low, murmuring voice was heard to rise and take on an affectionate tone, that person was seeking to mollify the other, and when the other voice rose in turn, that meant the tables had turned, and this time it was the former who was being talked down, and in the meantime, up until the point when you slid into sleep as though falling into a sudden abyss, you lay in your room becoming less and less able to distinguish between the sounds of an argument and the sounds of making up, of low laughter and shared sighs.

Now you're sitting at the table by the door to the gymnasium.

Your ledger is lying open on the left-hand side of the table, and your eyes are scanning the column of names, numbers, phone numbers, and addresses, checking you have the correct details before writing them in big letters on A4 paper. Jin-su said you have to make sure that you're able to contact the bereaved, even if every last one of the civilian militia were to die this very night. There's no one to help you write them up and fix them to coffins; you'll have to hurry if you're going to get them all done by six o'clock.

You hear someone calling your name.

You look up to see your mother emerge from between two trucks. As she approaches, you see that your middle brother isn't with her this time. Her gray blouse and baggy black trousers are the ones she wears whenever she goes to work in the shop, almost a kind of uniform. She looks as she always does, except for the fact that her hair, usually neatly combed, has suffered from the rain shower earlier.

You stand up and run forward, so glad to see her that you don't realize what you're doing until you're halfway down the steps. You stop short, confused, and your mother scurries up to grab your hand before you have time to retreat back to the safety of the gym.

"Let's go home," she says. You give your wrist a violent wrench, trying to shake free of her grip. The insistent, desperate strength in that grip is frightening, somehow, making you think of someone drowning. You have to use your other hand to pry her fingers away, one by one. "The army is coming. Let's go home, now."

Eventually you manage to shake her off, and lose no time in slipping back inside the building. Your mother tries to follow you in, but gets brought up short by the snaking queue of the bereaved, who are waiting to carry their coffins home with them.

You turn around and call back to her: "We're going to close up here at six, Mum."

Agitated, she moves from one foot to the other, trying to catch your eye from the other side of the line. You can only see her forehead, its furrows reminding you of a crying baby.

You call again, louder this time: "Once we've closed up, I'll come home. I promise."

Only then do those furrows smooth out.

"Make sure you do," she says. "Be back before the sun sets. We'll all have dinner together."

It's not been an hour since your mother left when you spot an old man heading slowly in your direction. You stand up. Even from this distance, his old-fashioned brown jacket has clearly seen better days. Dazzlingly white hair protrudes from beneath an ink-black peaked cap, and he leans heavily on a wooden walking stick as he totters forward. After weighting down the scraps of paper with the ledger and pen to stop them from being scattered by the wind, you walk down the steps.

"Who have you come to look for, sir?"

"My son and granddaughter," he says. He seems to be missing several teeth, which doesn't exactly help you puzzle out his thick accent.

"I got a lift on a cultivator over from Hwasun. They stopped us in the suburbs, said we couldn't come into the city, so I found a path over the mountains that the soldiers weren't guarding. I only just made it."

He takes a deep breath. The drops of saliva clinging to the sparse white hairs around his mouth are the color of ash. You can't understand how this elderly man, who finds even flat ground a challenge, managed to get here through the mountains.

"Our youngest boy, he's a mute . . . he had a fever when he was little, you see. Never spoke after that. A few days ago, someone who'd fled the city told me the soldiers had clubbed a mute to death, a while ago already now."

You take the old man by the arm and help him up the steps.

"Our eldest lad's daughter is renting a room near Jeonnam University while she's studying, so I went there yesterday evening and it was 'whereabouts unknown' . . . the landlord hasn't seen her for a good few days now, and the neighbors said the same."

You step into the gym hall and put on your mask. The women wearing mourning clothes are wrapping up the drinks bottles, newspapers, ice bags, and portrait photos in carrying cloths. There are also families arguing back and forth over whether to transfer their coffin to a safe home or just leave it where it is.

Now the old man extricates his arm from yours, declining your offer of assistance. He walks in front, holding a crumpled cloth to his nose. He examines the faces that are exposed one by one. He shakes his head. The rubber-covered gym floor turns the regular clack of his cane into a dull thump.

"What about those over there? Why're their faces hidden?" he asks, pointing toward the ones with cloths drawn up over their heads.

You hesitate, lips twitching at the deep sense of dread this question never fails to thud into you. You're waiting for those cotton shrouds, their white fibers stained with blood and watery discharge, to be peeled back; waiting to see again those faces torn lengthwise, shoulders gashed open, breasts decomposing inside blouses. At night, snatching a couple of hours' sleep hunched up on a chair in the basement cafeteria, your eyes start open at the vivid horror of those images. Your body twists and jerks as you feel a phantom bayonet stabbing into your face, your chest.

You lead the way over to the corner, battling against the resistance embedded deep in your muscles, that feeling of being tugged backward by some kind of huge magnet. You have to lean forward as you walk if you're to master it. Bending down to remove the cloth, your gaze is arrested by the sight of the translucent candle wax creeping down below the bluish flame.

How long do souls linger by the side of their bodies?

Do they really flutter away like some kind of bird? Is that what trembles the edges of the candle flame?

If only your eyesight was worse, so anything close up would be nothing more than a vague, forgiving blur. But there is nothing vague about what you have to face now. You don't permit yourself the relief of closing your eyes as you peel back the cloth, or even afterward, when you draw it back up again. You press your lips together so hard the blood shows through, clench your teeth, and think, *I would have run away.* Had it been this woman and not Jeong-dae who toppled over in front of you, still you would have run away. Even if it had been one of your brothers, your father, your mother, still you would have run away.

You look around at the old man. You don't ask him if this is his granddaughter. You wait, patiently, for him to speak when he's ready. *There will be no forgiveness.* You look into his eyes, which are flinching from the sight laid out in front of them as though it is the most appalling thing in all this world. *There will be no forgiveness. Least of all for me.*

2

The Boy's Friend, 1980

O ur bodies are piled on top of each other in the shape of a cross.

The body of a man I don't know has been thrown across my stomach at a ninety-degree angle, face up, and on top of him a boy, older than me, tall enough that the crook of his knees presses down onto my bare feet. The boy's hair brushed my face. I was able to see all of that because I was still stuck fast to my body, then.

They came toward us. Helmets, Red Cross armbands over the sleeves of mottled uniforms, quickly. Working in pairs, they began to lift us up and toss us into a military truck. An action as mechanical as loading sacks of grain. I hovered around my cheeks, the nape of my neck, clinging to these contours so as not to be parted from my body. Strangely, I found myself alone in the truck. There were the bodies, of course, but I didn't meet any others like me. They were there, perhaps, pressing close in the confines of the truck, but I couldn't see them, couldn't feel them. "We'll meet in the next world," people used to say. Those words were meaningless now.

The random jumble of bodies, mine included, were jolted along in the truck. Even after I'd lost so much blood that my heart finally stopped, the blood had continued to drain from my body, leaving the skin of my face as thin and transparent as writing paper. How strange, to see my own eyes shuttered in that blood-leached face.

As evening drew in around us, the truck left the built-up districts and raced down a deserted street, surrounded on both sides by darkening fields. It began to ascend a low hill, thickly wooded with tall oaks, then an iron gate swung into view. The truck slowed to a stop in front of the gate, and the two sentries saluted. Two long, sharp shrieks of metal, first when the sentries opened the gate, and again when they closed it behind us. The truck drove a little farther up the hill, turned into a clearing flanked by a low concrete building on one side and the oak wood on the other. It stopped.

They climbed down from the truck, walked around to the back, and undid the catch. Again in pairs, one person to seize the legs and the other to hold the arms, they moved us from the truck to the center of the clearing. My body seemed to slide beneath my wavering grasp, as though trying to shuck me off, but I clung on with a strength born of desperation. I looked up at the low building, the lighted windows. I wanted to know what kind of building it was, where I was, where my body was being taken.

They pushed their way into the thicket, which backed on to the empty lot. Following the gestured instructions of one who looked to be in charge, they stacked the bodies in the neat shape of a cross. Mine was second from the bottom, jammed in tight and crushed still flatter by every body that was piled on top. Even this pressure didn't squeeze any more blood from my wounds, which could only mean that it had all leaked out already. With my head tipped backward, the shade of the wood turned my face into a pallid ghost of itself, eyes closed and mouth hanging half open. When they threw a straw sack over the body of the man at the very top, the tower of bodies was transformed into the corpse of some enormous, fantastical beast, its dozens of legs splayed out beneath it.

After they left, the darkness closed in around us. The faint afterglow that had lingered in the western sky dissolved slowly into the surrounding blackness. I moved quickly up to the top of the tower of bodies, anchoring myself to that final man to watch a pale light seep through wisps of gray cloud, a shroud for the half-moon. The leaves and branches of the thicket intersected that light, their shadows throwing patterns on the dead faces like ghastly tattoos.

It must have been about midnight when I felt it touch me—that breath-soft slip of incorporeal something, that faceless shadow, lacking even language, now, to give it body. I waited for a while in doubt and ignorance, of who it was, of how to communicate with it. No one had ever taught me how to address a person's soul.

And perhaps, or so it seemed, my companion was equally baffled. Without the familiar bulwark of language, still we sensed, as a physical force, our existence in the mind of the other. When, eventually, I felt him sigh away, his resignation, his abandonment, left me alone again.

The night deepened, became threaded through with a string of similar occurrences. My shadow's edges became aware of a quiet touch; the presence of another soul. We would lose ourselves in wondering who the other was, without hands, feet, face, tongue, our shadows touching but never quite mingling. Sad flames licking up against a smooth wall of glass, only to wordlessly slide away, outdone by whatever barrier was there. Every time I felt a shadow slip from me, I looked up at the night sky. How I wanted to believe that cloud-wrapped half-moon was watching over me, an eye bright with intelligence—in reality nothing more than a huge, desolate lump of rock, utterly inert.

It was as that strange, vivid night was drawing to a close, as the faint blue light of dawn had begun to seep into the sky's black ink, that I suddenly thought of you, Dong-ho. Yes, you'd been there with me, that day. Until something like a cold cudgel had suddenly slammed into my side. Until I collapsed like a rag doll. Until my arms flung themselves up in mute alarm, amid the cacophony of footsteps drumming against the tarmac, ear-splitting gunfire. Until I felt the warm spread of my own blood moving up over my shoulder, the back of my neck. Until then, you were with me.

The grasshoppers were chirring. Hidden birds began to trill their morning song. Gusts of wind grazed the leaves of dark trees. The pale sun trembled over the lip of the horizon, moving up to the sky's center in a violent, majestic advance. Piled up behind the thicket, our bodies now began to soften in the sun, with putrefaction setting in. Clouds of gadflies and mayflies alighted on those places that were clotted with dried black blood, rubbed their front legs, crawled about, flew up, then settled again. I pushed out to the edges of my body, wanting to check whether yours was also jammed into the tower somewhere, whether you had been one of those souls whose fleeting caress had swept over me the previous night. But I couldn't, I was stuck, unable to detach myself from my body, which seemed to have acquired some kind of magnetic force. Unable to look away from my ghost-pale face.

Things went on like this until, with the sun almost at its zenith, I knew: you weren't there.

Not just that you weren't there, in that pile; you were still alive. For some reason, though the identities of the other souls who were clustered near at hand remained unknown, if I used all my powers of concentration to picture a specific individual, someone I'd known, I was able to tell whether or not they had died. And yet, at that moment, my discovery brought me no comfort. Instead, it frightened me to think that here by this strange thicket, surrounded by bodies gradually breaking down into their constituent parts, I was alone among strangers.

There was worse to come.

In an attempt to batten down the rising tide of fear, I thought of my sister. Watching the blazing sun describing an arc farther and farther to the south, staring at my face as though trying to bore through those shuttered eyelids, I thought of my sister, only of her. And I felt an agony that almost broke me. She was dead; she had died even before I had. With neither tongue nor voice to carry it, my scream leaked out from me in a mess of blood and watery discharge. My soul-self had no eyes; where was the blood coming from, what nerve endings were sparking this pain? I stared at my unchanging face. My filthy hands were as still as ever. Over my fingernails, dyed a deep rust by watery blood, red ants were crawling, silent.

●　●　●

I no longer felt fifteen. Thirty-five, forty-five; these numbers came, in turn, to feel somehow insufficient. Not even sixty-five, no, nor seventy-five, seemed to encompass what I was.

I wasn't Jeong-dae anymore, the runt of the year. I wasn't Park Jeong-dae, whose ideas of love and fear were both bound up in the figure of his sister. A strange violence welled up within me, not spurred by the fact of my death, but simply because of the thoughts that wouldn't stop tearing through me, the things I needed to know. Who killed me, who killed my sister, and why? The more of myself I devoted to these questions, the firmer this new strength within me became. The ceaseless flow of blood, blood that flowed from a place without eyes or cheeks, darkened, thickened, into a viscous treacle ooze.

My sister's soul, like mine, must still be lingering somewhere; but where? Now there were no such things as bodies for us; presumably physical proximity was no longer necessary for the two of us to meet. But without bodies, how would we know each other? Would I still recognize my sister as a shadow?

My body continued to putrefy. More and more mayflies crowded inside my open wounds. Gadflies crawled slowly over my lips and eyelids, rubbing their dark, slender legs together. Around the time when the day grew dark, and beams of orange light strafed down through the crowns of the oaks, exhausted with wondering where my sister might be, my thoughts turned instead to them. To the person who had killed me, and the one who had killed her. Where were they, right now? Even if they hadn't died, they would still have souls, so surely, if I bent all my thought on the idea of them, I would be able to sense them, touch them. I wanted to shuck off my body as a snake sheds its skin. I wanted to sever the pure strength, that force thin and taut as a spider's web, dilating and contracting, from the inert lump of rotting flesh. I wanted to be free to fly to wherever they were, and to demand of them, why did you kill me? Why did you kill my sister, what did you do to her?

The metal screech of the iron gate opening and then closing sliced through the silence of the night. The sound of an engine rumbled closer. The twin beams from the truck's headlights swept in sharply. When these beams arced over our bodies, the shadows cast by the leaves and branches, those black tattoos, danced over every face.

This time there were only two of them. They carried the latest batch of bodies over toward us, one by one. There were five altogether: four whose skulls had been caved in by some blunt weapon, leaving a splatter-pattern on their upper bodies, and one wearing a blue-striped hospital gown. They stacked them in a low heap next to ours, again in the shape of a cross. The body in the hospital gown was the last on, then they covered the pile with a straw sack and hurried away. I stared hard at their furrowed brows, their empty eyes, and realized that, in the space of a single day, our bodies had started to give off a horrific stench.

While they started the truck's engine, I slipped toward those new bodies. I wasn't alone; clustering around these new arrivals, I sensed the shadows of other souls. The four whose skulls had been staved in were three men and a woman. Thin, watery blood was still trickling from their clothes. Perhaps someone had splashed water over their heads, as their faces seemed relatively clean, compared with the state of their bodies. The young man in the hospital uniform was clearly set apart, special. Lying there with the straw sack pulled up to his chest like a quilt, he was cleaner and neater than any of the others. Someone had washed his body.

Someone had sutured his wounds and applied a poultice. The bandage coiled around his head gleamed white in the darkness. We were bodies, dead bodies, and in that sense there was nothing to choose between us. All the same, there was something infinitely noble about how his body still bore the traces of hands that had touched it, a tangible record of having been cared for, been valued, that made me envious and sad. Mine, on the other hand, crushed out of shape beneath a tower of others, was shameful, detestable.

From that moment on, I was filled with hatred for my body. Our bodies, tossed there like lumps of meat. Our filthy, rotting faces, reeking in the sun.

If I could close my eyes.

If I could escape the sight of our bodies, that festering flesh now fused into a single mass, like the rotting carcass of some many-legged monster. If I could sleep, truly sleep, not this flickering haze of wakefulness. If I could plunge headlong down to the floor of my pitch-dark consciousness.

If I could hide in dreams.

Or perhaps in memories.

If I could go back to last summer, waiting in the corridor for your class to be let out, jigging impatiently from one foot to the other. To the moment I saw your form teacher step out into the corridor and hastily straightened my uniform. To the moment after I'd watched all the other kids but you file out, when I stepped into the classroom and saw you rubbing away at the blackboard.

"What're you doing?"

"It's my turn this week."

"Like it was last week, you mean?"

"Well, it was meant to be someone else this time, but he had a blind date so I swapped with him."

"Dummy."

The moment our eyes met and we laughed, carefree. The moment the chalk dust got up my nose and threatened to provoke a sneezing fit. The moment I stealthily slipped the blackboard eraser you'd just finished shaking out into my bag. The moment I looked into your bewildered face and told my sister's story, without boasting, sadness, or embarrassment.

That night, I was lying down with the quilt pulled up to my stomach, pretending to sleep. My sister got home late from her shift like always, and I heard the familiar sounds of her setting up the table on the washstand and mixing water into her rice, which had gone cold. With my eyes open the barest chink in the darkness, I watched her, in profile, as she washed her hands, brushed her teeth, then tiptoed over to the window to check that the mosquito coil was burning properly. There, she discovered the blackboard eraser I'd balanced on the windowsill, and laughed— the first time low as a sigh, then a brief burst out loud a few moments later.

She shook her head, picked up the eraser, then quickly set it back down again. As usual, she spread her quilt out on the floor as far away from me as possible in the cramped space, but then crept over to where I was sleeping, shuffling on her knees. I shut my eyes fully, felt her hand pass once over my forehead, once over my cheeks, then heard her shuffle quietly back to her bedding, heard the quilt rustle as she slipped herself underneath. In the darkness, that laughter I'd heard from her just now sounded again. The first time low as a sigh, then a brief burst out loud a few moments later.

That was the memory I had to cling to, there in the pitch-dark thicket. I had to conjure up every little sensation of that night when I'd still had a body. The cold wind, heavy with moisture, that had blown in through the window late that night, the soft shush of it against the soles of my bare feet. The scent of lotion that rose faintly from the direction of my sleeping sister, mingled with menthol from the pain-relieving patches she applied to her aching shoulders and back. The grasshoppers in the yard, their faint, almost soundless cries. The hollyhocks that towered up in front of our room. The wild roses blooming in a gaudy, blowsy riot of color against the breeze-block wall opposite your room. My face, which my sister had twice caressed. My stilled, unseeing face, which she had loved.

I needed more memories.

I needed to keep spinning them out, quicker, in a continuous stream.

Summer nights, washing my neck and back in the yard. The rope of cold water you pumped into the metal pail, scattering into brilliant jewels as you splashed it over my sweat-gummed skin. Remember how you laughed, watching me shudder and *oooh*.

Riding my bike beside the river, racing along with the wind strong in my face, parting it before me like a ship's prow slicing through water. My white summer shirt flapping like a bird's wing. How I heard you call my name, riding along behind me, and responded by pumping the pedals as hard as I could. How I whooped with elation, hearing your plaintive voice fading away as I increased the distance between us.

It was a Sunday; in fact, it was Buddha's birthday. My sister and I were on our way to Gangjin for the day, to pay our respects to our mother at the temple where her spirit was worshipped. Springtime strips of rice paddy streaming by outside the window of the intercity bus. *Sis, the whole world is a fishbowl.* Clear water in the rice fields forming an unbroken mirror—it was just before planting season—reflecting nothing but an endless expanse of sky. The scent of acacia seeped in through the closed window, my nostrils twitching automatically.

Burning my tongue on a steamed potato my sister gave me, blowing on it hastily and juggling it in my mouth.

Flesh of a watermelon grainy as sugar, the glistening black seeds I didn't bother to pick out.

Racing back to the house where my sister was waiting, my jacket zipped up over a parcel of chrysanthemum bread, feet entirely numb with cold, the bread blazing hot against my heart.

Yearning to be taller.

To be able to do forty push-ups in a row.

For the time when I would hold a woman in my arms. That first woman who would permit such a liberty, whose face I didn't yet know, how I longed to extend my trembling fingers to the outer edge of her heart.

I think of the festering wound in my side.
Of the bullet that tore in there.
The strange chill, the seeming blunt force, of that initial impact,

That instantly became a lump of fire churning my insides,
Of the hole it made in my other side, where it flew out and
    tugged my hot blood behind it.
Of the barrel it was blasted out of.
Of the smooth trigger.
Of the eye that had me in its sights.
Of the eyes of the one who gave the order to fire.

I want to see their faces, to hover above their sleeping eyelids like a guttering flame, to slip inside their dreams, spend the nights flaring in through their forehead, their eyelids. Until their nightmares are filled with my eyes, my eyes as the blood drains out. Until they hear my voice asking, demanding, why.

The days and nights that passed then did so without note. A succession of dawns and dusks went by, each half-light the selfsame shade of blue. The passage of time was otherwise marked only by the sound of the military truck's engine, a deep rumble in the dead of each night, its headlamps' twin beams slicing through the darkness.

Every time they came by, the tower of bodies covered by the straw sack would be added to. Bodies with their skulls crushed and cratered, shoulders dislocated, rather than having been shot. And now and then, bodies that still appeared relatively intact, dressed carefully in neat hospital gowns, and swathed in bandages.

On one occasion, the bodies of ten people they'd just piled up seemed to be missing their heads. At first I thought they'd been decapitated; then I realized that, in fact, their faces had been covered in white paint, erased. I swiftly shrank back. Necks tipped back, those dazzlingly white faces were angled toward the thicket. Staring out into the empty air, their features a perfect blank.

Had these bodies all been packed into that street?

Had they been there alongside me, jostling my elbow, part of that vast mass of humanity whose voices ebbed and surged as one, yelling and singing and cheering at the buses and taxis that inched their way through the throng, headlights on, making a show of solidarity?

What happened to the bodies of the two men who'd been gunned down in front of the station, which some of the protesters loaded into a handcart to push at the head of the column? What happened to those two pairs of feet bouncing gently in the air, almost unseemly in their nakedness? I saw a shudder run through you the moment you spotted them. You blinked violently, your eyelashes fluttering in agitation. I grasped your hand and tugged you forward, toward the head of the column, while you muttered to yourself in blank incomprehension, *our soldiers are shooting. They're shooting at us.* I pulled you toward them with all my strength, opening my throat to sing while you seemed on the point of tears. I sang along with the national anthem, my heart fit to burst. Before they sent that white-hot bullet driving into my side. Before those faces were canceled out, expunged by white paint.

The rot ran quickest in the bodies at the base of the tower, white grubs burrowing into them until not an inch of skin was left untouched. I looked on in silence as my face blackened and swelled, my features turned into festering ulcers, the contours that had defined me, that had given me clear edges, crumbled into ambiguity, leaving nothing that could be recognized as me.

As the nights wore on, increasingly more shadows came and pressed up against my own. Our encounters were, as always, poorly improvised things. We were never able to tell who the other was, but could vaguely surmise how long we'd been together for. When a shadow that had been there from the first, and one that was newly arrived, both came to touch my own, extending along flat planes and folding over edges, I was somehow able to distinguish between them, though I couldn't have said how. Certain shadows seemed marked by the weight of long drawn-out agonies, whose depths I was unable to fathom. Were these the souls of those bodies whose clothes were roughly torn, who bore deep purple bruises beneath each fingernail? Every time our shadow-boundaries brushed against each other, an echo of some appalling suffering was transmitted to me like an electric shock.

If we'd been given a little more time, might we have arrived, eventually, at a moment of understanding? Might we have groped our way toward exchanging a few words, or thoughts?

But this thread of quiet nights and days was severed.

That day, the rain bucketed down all through the afternoon. The sheer force of it sluiced the caked blood off our bodies, and the rot ran even quicker after this ablution. Our blue-black faces gleamed dully in the light of the full moon.

This time, they arrived earlier than usual, before midnight. As I always did at the sound of their approach, I angled myself away from the tower of bodies and melded seamlessly with the shadows of the thicket. The past few days had always brought the same two people; this time, I immediately made out at least six figures. They gripped the new bodies roughly, carrying them over and piling them up in a much more slapdash manner than the usual neat cross shape. This done, they immediately drew back, covering their noses and mouths as though gagging on the stench, gazing at the tower of bodies with a vacant look in their eyes.

One of them went over to the truck and returned with a plastic can of petrol. His back, shoulders, and arms tensed up as he struggled under the load, staggering toward our bodies.

This is it, I thought. A multitude of shadows quivered all around, grazing my own and each other's with soft shudders. Trembled meetings in the empty air, instantly dispersing, edges overlapping again, a soundless, fluttering agitation.

Two of the soldiers who'd been standing back came forward and took the plastic can between them. Working calmly and methodically, they removed the lid and began to pour the petrol over the towers of bodies. Making sure that each was evenly covered, that no body got more or less than its fair share. Only after shaking the last drops out of the can did they draw back to a safe distance. Each of them broke off a piece of dried shrubbery, sparked their lighters, and, once the flame had caught, hurled it forward with all their strength.

The blood-stiffened clothes, their rotting fibers matted to our flesh, were the first to burst into flame. After that, the flames ate steadily through the head's thick hair, the fine down covering the body, then fat, muscle, and innards. The blaze roared up as though threatening to engulf the wood. It was as bright in the clearing as it was in broad daylight.

It was then I realized that what had been binding us to this place was none other than that flesh, that hair, those muscles, those organs. The magnetic force holding us to our bodies rapidly began to lose its strength. At first shrinking back into the thicket, we slipped past each other's shadows, passing over and under like a caress, until finally, clinging to the heavy clots of black smoke being belched from our bodies, we soared up into the air as though exhaled in a single breath.

The soldiers began to return to the truck—all but two, who, seemingly having been ordered to stay and watch until the very end, remained in their places, standing at attention. I skimmed down toward them, flickering around their necks and shoulders, where one bore the insignia of a private first class, the other that of a sergeant. I peered into their faces. How young they were. How their black pupils, dilated with fear, reflected the bonfire of our bodies.

The sparks spat out from the blaze snapped like fireworks. Water in the viscera hissed and boiled, until the organs dried and shriveled. Black smoke rolled off our rotten bodies in ragged, intermittent breaths, and in those places where there was nothing left to produce it the white gleam of bone was revealed. Those souls whose bodies had already been thus reduced drifted farther away, their wavering shadows no longer sensed. And so eventually we were free, free to go wherever we would.

Where shall I go? I asked myself.

To your sister.

But where is she?

I made an effort to keep calm. My body was at the very bottom of the tower, so there was still some time before the fire consumed it.

Go to those who killed you, then.

But where are they?

The wood's inky shadows dappled the damp, sandy soil of the clearing. I flickered amid those patches of light and shade, thinking where should I go, how do I get there? I should have been grateful, perhaps, for the ease, the neatness with which my blackened, rotted face would disappear. The body that had caused me such shame was going to be devoured by the flames—that was no cause for regret. I wanted to pare myself down to a simpler existence, just as I had while I'd still been alive. I was determined not to be afraid of anything.

I'll go to you.

And just like that, everything became clear.

There was no hurry. As long as I set out before the sun came up, I'd be able to find my way to the heart of the city by the lights in the windows. I'd be able to grope my way through the lightening streets, to the house where you and I used to live. Perhaps you'd found my sister in the meantime. Perhaps I'd be able to greet her again, in the only way left to me—by haunting the edges of her body. Or no, maybe she was already back there, in the room we used to share, waiting for me, hovering by the window, or above that cold stone terrace.

I slipped between the fire's orange flames as it burned itself out. The tower of bodies collapsed into an indistinguishable heap of glowing embers, bodies formerly separate now mingled together.

The fire subsided, and darkness crept back into the woods.

The young soldiers were kneeling in the dirt, propping each other up shoulder to shoulder, sleeping like the dead.

It was then that I heard it: an almighty thunderclap, like thousands of fireworks going off at once. A distant scream. Living breaths snapped like a neck. Souls shocked from their bodies.

That was when you died, Dong-ho.

I didn't know where, I only knew that was what it was: the moment of your death.

I whirled up and up through the lightless sky. It was pitch dark. Nowhere in the city, not a single district, not even a single house, had their lights on. There was only one, distant point of light, where I saw a succession of flares shooting up, glittering shards of light being scattered from the barrels of guns.

Should I have gone there, right then? If I had, would I have been able to find you, Dong-ho, to ease the terror you must have felt at having just been knocked from your body? With that thick, heavy blood still creeping from my shadow-eyes, amid the dawn light being calved from the night slow as an iceberg, I found it impossible to move.

3

The Editor, 1985

At four o'clock on a Wednesday afternoon, the editor Kim Eun-sook received seven slaps to her right cheek. She was struck so hard, over and over in the exact same spot, that the capillaries laced over her right cheekbone burst, the blood trickling out through her torn skin. How many slaps had it taken before that happened? She couldn't be sure. Wiping the smear of blood away with the palm of her hand, she stepped out into the street. The late November air was crisp and clear. About to walk onto the pedestrian crossing, she paused, wondering whether it would be wise to go back to the office. The stretched skin was tightening over her rapidly swelling cheek. She had gone deaf in her right ear. One more slap and her eardrum might have burst. She swallowed the metallic blood that had gathered along her gums, and turned toward the bus stop that would take her home.

Slap One

Now begins the process of forgetting the seven slaps. One per day, then it'll be over and done within a week. Today, then, is that first day.

She turns the key in the lock and steps inside her rented room. She removes her shoes and lines them up neatly, then lies down on the floor, on her side, without even bothering to unbutton her coat. She rests her left cheek on her folded arms. The right cheek is still swelling. The upward pressure prevents her from opening her right eye properly. The toothache that had begun in her upper molars throbs up to her temples.

After lying in the same position for close to twenty minutes, she gets up. Stripping down to her white underwear, she hangs up her clothes, slides her feet into her slippers, and shuffles out to the washroom. A scoop of cold water from the washbowl to splash onto her swollen face. She opens her mouth as far as she can manage, and brushes her teeth so gently it's more like a caress. The phone rings, then cuts off. She dries her wet feet with the towel, and as soon as she steps back into the room the phone rings again. She reaches out to pick up the receiver, then changes her mind and yanks the cord out at the wall.

"What will happen if I answer?" she mumbles to herself, rolling out the thin mattress and cotton quilt. She isn't hungry. She could force herself to eat something, but it would only give her indigestion. It's cold under the quilt, and she huddles into a ball. That phone call just now would have been from the office; probably the boss. She would have to answer his questions. *I'm okay, it's just that they hit me. No, only slaps. I can still come to work. I'm okay, I don't need to go to the hospital. My face is a bit swollen, that's all.* Good thing she'd pulled the cord out.

As the quilt's cocoon starts to warm up, she cautiously straightens out. Outside the window, it is six o'clock and already dark. The light from the streetlamp glows dully orange through a section of the glass. Once her tension has dissipated a little thanks to the warmth and her comfortable position, she turns her mind to the task at hand.

Now, how am I going to forget the first slap?

When the man struck her the first time, she didn't make a sound. Neither did she cringe away in anticipation of the next slap. Rather than jumping up from her seat, hiding under the interrogation room's table, or running to the door, she waited quietly, holding her breath. Waited for the man to stop, to stop hitting her. The second time, the third time, even the fourth time she told herself would surely be the last. Only when the palm of his hand came flying toward her face for the fifth time did she think, *he's not going to stop, he's just going to keep on hitting me.* After the sixth time, she wasn't thinking anything anymore. She'd stopped counting. But when the last slap had been delivered and the man plumped down across the table from her, lolling against the back of the folding chair, she silently added another two to her mental tally. Seven.

His face was utterly ordinary. Thin lips, no noticeable irregularities to his features. He wore a pale yellow shirt with a wide collar, and his gray suit trousers were held up by a belt. Its buckle gleamed. Had they met by chance in the street, she would have taken him for some run-of-the-mill company manager or section chief.

"Bitch. A bitch like you, in a place like this? Anything could happen, and no one would find out."

At this point, the force of the slap had already burst the capillaries in her cheek, and the man's fingernails had broken her skin. But Eun-sook hadn't known that yet. She stared blankly across at the man's face. "Listen to what I'm telling you, if you don't want to die in some ditch where not even the rats and crows will find you. Tell me where that bastard is."

She had met up with the translator—"that bastard"—a fortnight ago, at a bakery by Cheonggye stream. It was the day the weather had suddenly changed; she remembered having to rummage through her winter clothes to find a sweater to go out in. She used a napkin to blot away the wet patch left by the cup of barley tea, then placed the proofs on the table, facing the translator. *Take your time, sir.* While she occupied herself with tearing off pieces of the crunchy streusel bread, washing each mouthful down with a sip of cold tea, he went through the manuscript with a fine-tooth comb. He took almost an hour all told, occasionally asking her opinion on minor amendments and additions. Lastly, he suggested that they go through the table of contents together. She brought her chair around to his side of the table and went through the proofs page by page, double-checking the amendments and table of contents. Before they parted, she asked how she should contact him when the book came out. He smiled.

"I'll go and look for it in a bookshop."

She took an envelope out of her bag and held it out to him.

"It's the royalties for the first edition. The boss said he wanted you to have it in advance." The translator took the envelope without speaking, and slid it into the inner pocket of his jacket. "How shall we get any further royalties to you?"

"I'll be in touch, later on."

The impression he'd given was far removed from that of a wanted criminal. If anything, he'd come across as somewhat timid. His skin had had a yellowish cast, hinting at some problem with his liver, though perhaps it was simply due to having spent so much time indoors. The same went for his paunch and fleshy jaw. "I'm very sorry, making you come all this way on such a cold day." She'd smiled inwardly at such unwarranted courtesy from someone who was by far her senior.

"This was in your drawer, you little slut . . . that bastard wrote it, and you're telling me you don't know where he is?"

Avoiding the man's eyes as he flung the bundle of proofs onto the table, she looked up instead at the dusty tube of the fluorescent lamp. *He's going to hit me again*, she thought, and blinked.

She had no idea what made her think of the fountain at just that moment. Behind her closed eyelids, glittering jets of water sprayed up into the June sky. Eighteen years old and passing by on the bus, she'd screwed her eyes tight shut. Glancing off one droplet after another, sharp little shards of sunlight burrowed through her heat-flushed eyelids, stinging her pupils. She got off the bus at the stop in front of her house and went straight to the public phone booth. Shrugging her satchel onto the floor, she swiped at the sweat trickling down over her forehead, inserted a coin into the slot, dialed 114, and waited. "The Provincial Office complaints department, please." She dialed the number she was given and waited again. "I've just seen water coming out of the fountain, and I don't think it should be allowed." Tremulous at first, her voice became clearer as she carried on speaking. "What I mean is, how can it have started operating again already? It's been dry ever since the uprising began and now it's back on again, as though everything's back to normal. How can that be possible?"

• • •

"Why give his contact details to some assistant editor he's never met before, when even his own family don't know how to get in touch with him?"

Blinking rapidly, she managed to say that she doesn't know, she honestly doesn't know.

He slammed his fist down on the table and she recoiled, her hand automatically flinching up to her cheek, as though she'd been hit again. And only then, upon lowering her hand, did she stare in surprise at her bloodied palm.

How am I going to forget? she wonders, in the darkness.

How can I forget that first slap?

The eyes of the man, who had examined her in silence at first, calm and composed like someone about to carry out an entirely practical item of business.

Herself, who, when he'd raised his hand, had sat there thinking, *surely he's not going to hit me.*

The first blow, that had seemed to jolt her neck out of alignment.

Slap Two

The publisher's niece, a lively, cheerful young woman who frequently ran errands for them, dropped by the office just before lunch.

"Ah, there you are!" Her uncle greeted her warmly, but darted a hurried glance over at Eun-sook when the latter looked up from the papers she'd been examining.

"Have the bound proofs arrived yet?" Eun-sook asked, smiling stiffly. Unable to tear her gaze from the older woman's face, the publisher's niece fumbled with her briefcase, eventually tugging out a proof.

"What happened to your face?" When this met with no response, the young woman cornered Yoon, who dealt with production, and asked again. "What happened to Eun-sook's face?" Yoon merely shook his head; the young woman's eyes widened, and she turned back to the publisher.

"Well," he said, "I told Eun-sook she should go home early today, but what can I say, she's a stubborn one . . ."

He tapped a cigarette out of his pack, stuck it between his lips and lit up. Opening the window behind his chair, he stuck his head through the gap and took such a deep drag on the cigarette that his cheeks caved right in, then finally blew out the smoke. He was middle-aged, the sort of man whom even the smartest clothes couldn't prevent from looking permanently wrung-out. A man who used humble, honorific language even to those who were young enough to be his children. A man who, despite being the head of this tiny publishing house, hated the title "Boss" and wouldn't allow anyone to address him as anything other than "Publisher" to his face. The high-school classmate of the translator whose whereabouts the police detective had demanded from her.

The owner's niece left once she'd finished talking with Eun-sook, leaving the mood in the office somewhat deflated. The boss stubbed out his cigarette.

"Do you fancy some barbecue for lunch, Miss Kim? My treat. Beef skirt from that place up by the junction."

This sudden show of sociability chimed oddly with Eun-sook. It hadn't occurred to her to wonder before, but now she began to doubt. The boss had also stopped in at Seodaemun police station, early yesterday afternoon—not that long before she had. How had he persuaded them to leave him alone?

"Thank you for the offer, but I'm fine with getting something myself." Her answer might have seemed a little frosty, but she couldn't really help that given that her swollen face hurt too much for her to smile. "You know I don't like meat."

"Ah yes, that's right, you're not a meat fan." The boss nodded to himself.

It wasn't so much eating meat that Eun-sook disliked; what really turned her stomach was watching it cook on the hot plate. When the blood and juices rose to the surface, she had to look away. When a fish was being griddled with the head still attached. That moment when moisture formed on the frozen eyeballs as they thawed in the pan, when a watery fluid flecked with gray scum dribbled out of its gaping mouth, that moment when it always seemed to her as though the dead fish was trying to say something. She always had to avert her eyes.

"So then, what shall it be? What would you like to eat, Miss Kim?"

Yoon chose that moment to pipe up.

"You'll bend our ears for us if we go somewhere expensive and run up a huge bill. Let's go to that café we went to last time."

With Yoon making three the office would be empty, so they locked the door behind them before walking up to the café by the junction. It was next door to the barbecue place the boss had originally suggested—a fairly ramshackle place, where home-style boiled rice was dished up by a proprietor whose summer flip-flops exposed a toenail black with rot, then in winter she shuffled around with grubby socks stuffed into tatty old snow boots.

As they were finishing their meal, the boss turned to Eun-sook.

"Shall I stop by the censor's office tomorrow?"

"That's always been my job . . ."

"Well, there was a lot of hassle yesterday; I'm just sorry you had to be involved in that."

She looked across at him, pondering his words. How had he contrived to come out of there unharmed? By sticking only to what were, strictly speaking, the facts? *Kim Eun-sook is the editor in charge. The two of them met at the bakery by Cheonggye stream and went through the manuscript proofs. That's all I know.* He'd stuck to the facts, nothing wrong with that; but was that bitter thing called conscience quietly needling away inside him?

"It's always been my job," Eun-sook repeated, but firmer this time. She attempted a smile but the pain rendered it a sorry affair, and she twisted away to save the boss from being troubled by the sight of her swollen cheek.

Once everyone else had left the office and headed home, Eun-sook wound her ink-black scarf around the lower portion of her face, making sure that her cheeks were covered all the way up to her eyes. She gave the kerosene stove one last double-check, switched off all the lights, and even flicked the fuses to the down position. Standing before the door, its glass darkly mirroring the lightless office, she closed her eyes for just a moment, as though steeling herself before stepping outside.

The evening wind was bitter. It chilled the skin around her eyes, the only part left exposed by the scarf. Still, she didn't want to take the bus. After a day spent sitting at her desk, she took pleasure in an unhurried walk home through the streets. This was the only time of day when she chose not to shut out the inchoate thoughts that surfaced, unbidden, as she threaded her way through the streets.

Was it because he is left-handed that the man hit my right cheek with his left hand?

But when he tossed the proofs onto the table, when he handed me the pen, he definitely used his right hand . . .

Is it that the specific emotional rush when you attack someone sparks a reflexive response in the left hand rather than the right?

The bitter taste at the back of her mouth was identical to the bile that surfaced before a bout of carsickness. Swallowing saliva was her usual trick to quell this familiar nausea, the sensation occurring simultaneously in the back of her mouth, her throat, and stomach, and unaccountably tied to thoughts of you. Yet it wasn't enough, this time, so she got some gum out of her coat pocket and started to work it with her teeth.

Wasn't his hand a little on the small side, compared with most men?

She threaded her way between men in monochrome blazers, schoolgirls wearing white surgical masks, women whose skirt suits left their calves exposed to the biting wind, walking with her head bowed.

Wasn't it a hand like any other, not especially large or coarse, one you could see on any man?

She walked on, conscious of the scarf's slight pressure against the swelling. She walked on, the strong scent of acacia coming from the gum she made sure to keep on the left side of her mouth. Remembering how she had sat there, neither seeking to flee nor uttering the faintest cry of protest, merely waiting, holding her breath, for that second slap to come flying toward her face, she walked on.

Slap Three

She alights from the bus at the stop in front of Deoksu palace. Just like the day before, her scarf is wound around her face all the way up to her eyes. Beneath the scarf, the swelling has subsided, leaving in its place the clear imprint of a hand-sized reddish bruise.

"Excuse me." A robust-looking plainclothes policeman stops her in front of City Hall. "Please open your bag."

At such moments, she knows, a part of one's self must be temporarily detached from the whole. One level of her conscious mind peels away, a sheet of paper folding with the ease of habit along an oft-used crease. She opens her bag and displays the contents—a hand towel, acacia gum, a pencil case, the bound proof that the publisher's niece brought to the office the day before, Vaseline for chapped lips, a notebook, a purse—without the slightest flicker of shame.

"What is your business here?"

"I have an appointment at the censor's office. I work for a publisher." She looks the policeman directly in the eye.

She produces her resident's card when instructed to do so. She looks on, unmoving, as he rummages through the pouch containing her sanitary towels. Just like what had happened two days ago, in the interrogation room at the police station. Just like that sleet-streaked April four years ago, after her cramming had finally paid off, and she'd passed the university entrance exams second time around and moved up to Seoul from Gwangju.

She'd been eating lunch late in the university cafeteria when the glass door banged open and a crowd of students raced in. The hand clutching her spoon had frozen as she stared blankly at the sight of plainclothes policemen pursuing them through

the cafeteria, roaring threats and brandishing clubs. One of their
number seemed especially worked up—skidding to a halt in front
of a chubby boy whose mouth was hanging open above his plate
of curry and rice, he snatched up a chair and swung it over the
table. The burst of blood from the boy's forehead gushed down
over his nose and mouth. The spoon dropped from Eun-sook's
fingers. Unthinkingly bending down to pick it up, her hand closed
upon a flyer that had fallen to the floor. The thick font swam in
front of her eyes. DOWN WITH THE BUTCHER CHUN DOO-HWAN.
Just then, a rough hand grabbed hold of her long hair. It tore the
paper from her grasp and dragged her off her chair.

DOWN WITH THE BUTCHER CHUN DOO-HWAN.

Those words feel seared onto her chest as she gazes up now at
the photograph of the president hung on the plaster wall. *How is
it,* she wonders, *that a face can so effectively conceal what lies behind it?
How is it not indelibly marked by such callousness, brutality, murderous-
ness?* Perched awkwardly on a stool beneath the window, she tears
at a hangnail. The room is warm, but she can't remove her scarf;
the brand on her cheek is flushed from the radiator's heat.

The man behind the counter wears the uniform of the Defense
Security Command. When he calls the name of her publisher,
Eun-sook goes up to the counter and hands over the book proof.
She asks for the manuscript proofs to be returned, which she gave
in for inspection two weeks ago.

"Please wait here."

Beneath the murderer's framed photograph is a door with
frosted glass. Behind that door, she knows, the censors are busy
with their work. She pictures the scene: middle-aged inspectors

sporting army uniforms, their faces entirely unfamiliar, poring over the open books covering the table. The counter manager opens the door just as wide as he needs to in order to angle his body through, the movement swift and practiced. Barely three minutes have gone by before he returns to his post.

"Sign here, please." When he pushes the ledger toward her, she hesitates. A single glance had been sufficient to see that there was something strange about the manuscript proof he has just put down on the counter. "Sign, please."

Eun-sook signs her name, and is given the manuscript.

Any further exchange of words would be pointless. The censors' task has been carried out, and now Eun-sook holds the result in her hands.

She turns and walks away from the counter, her steps slow and almost stumbling. She comes to a halt by the row of benches and turns the pages of the manuscript. Having spent a full month typing it up, comparing it against the original and completing the third printer's proof, she knows its content practically by heart. Now at the final stage before publication, it only remains to be properly printed.

Her initial impression is that the pages have been burned. They've been thrown onto a fire and left to blacken, reduced to little more than a lump of coal.

Submitting the manuscript proofs to the censor's office, then calling back on the appointed day—she's been through this same process every month since starting work at the publisher's. After checking to see which sections of the text had been crossed out with a black line—usually three or four, a dozen at the most—she would return to the office feeling somewhat deflated, and send the corrected proofs off to the printers.

But this time is different. More than half of the sentences in the ten-page introduction have been scored through. In the thirty or so pages following, this percentage rises so that the vast majority of sentences have a line through them. From around the fiftieth page onward, perhaps because drawing a line had become too labor-intensive, entire pages have been blacked out, presumably using an ink roller. These saturated pages have left the manuscript bloated and distended, waterlogged flotsam washed up on some beach.

Handling it as though it really were charcoal, friable and likely to crumble, she slipped this alien object into her bag. Its leaden weight was entirely incommensurate with its actual substance. She cannot remember how she made it out of that office, how she walked down the corridor and out through the main doors, where a plainclothes policeman was standing guard.

There is no way, now, that this collection of plays can be published. All their efforts had been in vain, right from the start.

Her mind fumbles through those few, scattered sentences that were spared from the introduction.

After you were lost to us, all our hours declined into evening.

Evening are our streets and our houses.

In this half-light that no longer darkens nor lightens, we eat, and walk, and sleep.

She recalls sentences roughly darned and patched, places where the forms of words can just about be made out in paragraphs that had been otherwise expunged. *You. I. That. Perhaps. Precisely. Everything. You. Why. Gaze. Your eyes. Near and far. That. Vividly. Now. A little more. Vaguely. Why did you. Remember?* Gasping for breath in these interstices, tiny islands among language charred out of existence. How can there be water coming out of the fountain? What can we possibly be celebrating?

She turns her back on the black bronze statue of the general with his sword, and walks on without pausing. Her breathing constricted by the scarf, pain throbbing dully beneath the reddened skin of her exposed cheekbone, she walks on.

Slap Four

The editor Kim Eun-sook had sat there and waited for the man's hand. No, she had waited for him to stop. But really she hadn't been waiting for anything. She was simply struck in the face. The man beat her; she was beaten. And that, now, is what she has to forget. Today is the day for forgetting the fourth slap.

Just outside the office, at the end of the corridor, she turns on the tap at the washbasin and holds her hands under the cold water. Her wet fingers smooth her long hair, which curls without the need for a perm, and after she has succeeded in neatening it a little, she ties it up with a black rubber band.

She doesn't put on any makeup, just Vaseline for her chapped lips. Powdering one's face to a milky whiteness, spritzing on perfume, slipping feet into high-heeled shoes: these are all things that other women do, but not she. Today is a Saturday, meaning her working day finishes at 1 p.m., but she has no boyfriend to eat lunch with. During her brief time at university, she made no friends whom she could now arrange to see. Instead, she will do as she always does, which is to return quietly to her rented room. She will soak cold rice in warm water to soften it, eat, then go to sleep. While she sleeps she will forget the fourth slap.

The corridor is fairly gloomy even during the day. Hearing someone call her name, Eun-sook looks up. Whoever they are, they sound happy to see her. She soon recognizes the theater producer Mr. Seo striding toward her, backlit against the small window.

"How have you been, Eun-sook?"

Her response to this hearty greeting is a quiet "hello," and when she bows Mr. Seo's eyes widen visibly behind his brown-framed glasses.

"Goodness, what happened to your face?"

"I had a bit of an accident." She gives a half-smile.

"What kind of accident . . ." Seeing her hesitation, he swiftly changes the subject. "Is the boss in?"

"No, he didn't come in today. He said he had a wedding to attend."

"Is that so? I called him yesterday evening and he said he'd be here."

Eun-sook opens the door to the office.

"Please come in, sir."

Something twitches in her cheek as she leads him over to the table they use for receiving guests. She goes into the tiny kitchen and places her hands on both cheeks; the right one throbbing, the left, tensed. Taking a deep breath to compose herself, she heats up the coffeepot. She can't understand why her hands are shaking, as though she's been caught out in a lie. After all, it's not as though she's the one who destroyed that book. Why isn't the boss here? Has he deliberately stayed away in order to avoid this delicate situation?

"While we were on the phone yesterday evening and I asked how much they'd redacted, the boss just sighed," Mr. Seo tells

Eun-sook. She sets down his coffee and straightens the pale yellow tablecloth. "So I came to see for myself. Even if the book itself can't be published, that won't really affect the performance run. Any parts they had an issue with will just have to be fixed or taken out, and then they'll give us the go-ahead."

Eun-sook goes over to her desk and opens the bottom drawer. She takes out the manuscript proof, brings it back over to the table, and puts it down in front of Mr. Seo. As she sits, she sees his habitual friendly smile falter; he seems shocked, but quickly regains his composure. He examines each page of the manuscript, not even choosing to skip the ones that have been completely mulched by the ink roller.

"I'm sorry, sir," she says, watching his fingers tentatively brush the final page, where the copyright details are printed. "Truly sorry. I wish there was something I could say."

"Eun-sook." She meets his eyes. He looks baffled. "What's the matter?"

Startled, she scrubs hastily at her eyes. She had sat through that sequence of seven slaps without her eyes welling up, so she can't understand why it's happening now.

"I'm sorry," she repeats. The tears keep leaking out, faster than she can dash them away, like sticky sap oozing from a stem. "I'm truly sorry, sir."

"What do you have to be sorry for? Why should you apologize to me?"

Eun-sook's hand is hovering near her cup when Mr. Seo abruptly puts the manuscript down; she starts, spilling some coffee, and Mr. Seo's nimble fingers snatch the proof up again. To save it from getting stained. As though it still contains something. As though everything in it hasn't been nullified.

Slap Five

It was a Sunday, so Eun-sook had planned to sleep in. As always, though, her eyes were open before it was even 4 a.m.

She lay there in the darkness for a few moments, then got up and went to the kitchen. It seemed unlikely that she'd be able to get back to sleep, so she took a sip of cold water and then started on the laundry. Her socks, which were in an array of bright colors, her towel, and white shirts all went into the small washing machine, while she washed her underwear and dark gray sweater by hand, before spreading them out to dry on an upturned wicker basket. Her jeans went into the laundry basket; they might as well wait until she had more coloreds to wash. She hunkered down on the kitchen floor, letting the machine's rhythmic swoosh gradually lull her back to drowsiness.

Okay, time to sleep.

When she went back to her room, lay down, and forced her eyes shut, the unyielding stiffness of the mattress, of the paper-covered floor, passed through the edges of her body and leached into her muscles. It spread from her shoulders downward, leaving her paralyzed, unable even to moan. When this slow seepage stopped, in its place the space around her seemed to shrink, cement walls closing in on all sides.

She gasped for breath, and her eyes jerked open. She could tell from the sound that the washing machine was on its final spin cycle. After a few minutes, the swoosh of the rotating drum ceased as abruptly as a strangled breath, and a high-pitched bleep cut through the silence it had left in its wake.

Eun-sook stayed where she was. There were still three slaps that she needed to forget, and today was the turn of the fifth. The fifth slap, when she'd told herself to stop counting. The fifth slap, when it had felt as though the stinging flesh was peeling from her cheekbone, when blood had begun to seep to the surface of the skin.

She got to her feet and went to hang up the laundry, on the washing line strung above the sink. Even this task didn't take as long as she'd hoped, and the dawn was still far away when she went back to her bedroom.

She folded the quilt with exaggerated care and put it on top of the chest of drawers, organized her desk, and arranged the drawers, and still the day remained impossibly far away. She tidied everything that could be tidied, even lining up her toiletries on the side table. Briefly, she let her hand linger on the small mirror she kept there. The world imprisoned in its glass was cold, silent, and unchanging. Gazing abstractedly into that world, the face that looked out at her was familiar, but for the bluish bruise branded on the cheek.

There'd been a time when people had been quick to tell her how "cute" she was. *You've got such nice features, it's like they came out of a copybook. You look like a dancer with that black hair, a salon perm would be pointless on you.* But after that summer when she was eighteen, the summer of the fountain, no one said such things to her anymore. Now she was twenty-three, and loveliness was what was expected. Loveliness in the form of apple-red cheeks, of comely dimples expressing delight in life's brilliance. Yet Eun-sook herself wanted nothing more than to speed up the aging process. She wanted this damned, dreary life not to drag on too long.

She gave the room a thorough going-over with a damp cloth, making sure to get into all the nooks and crannies. But even after washing the cloth, hanging it up, and going back to sit at her desk, the nighttime stubbornly lingered. She didn't read anything, just tried to sit there quietly, and hunger began to creep up on her. She went and filled a bowl with some of the early-ripening rice that her mother had prepared for her, then brought it back to her desk. As she silently chewed the grains of rice, it occurred to her, as it had before, that there was something shameful about eating. Gripped by this familiar shame, she thought of the dead, for whom the absence of life meant they would never be hungry again. But life still lingered on for her, with hunger still a yoke around her neck. It was that which had tormented her for the past five years—that she could still feel hunger, still salivate at the sight of food.

"Can't you just put it behind you?" her mother had asked, that winter when she'd failed the university entrance exams and confined herself to the house. "This is hard on me, you know. Just forget about what happened, then you can go off to university like everyone else, earn a living and meet a nice man. . . . It'd be such a weight off my shoulders."

Not wanting to be a burden, Eun-sook had resumed her studies. She applied for a place at a university in Seoul, as far away from Gwangju as possible. Of course, Seoul was hardly a safe haven. Plainclothes policemen were a permanent feature of campus life, and students who fell foul of them were forcibly enlisted in the army and sent to the DMZ. The situation was so precarious that meetings frequently had to be called off. Life was a constant skirmish. The central library's glass windows were smashed from the inside so that banners could be hung from them. DOWN WITH THE BUTCHER CHUN DOO-HWAN. Some students even went so far as to secure a rope to one of the pillars on the roof, knot it around their waist, and then jump off. It was a tactic to gain time while the plainclothes policemen would be occupied in racing up to the roof and hauling up the rope. Until this happened, the student dangling at the end would scatter flyers and yell slogans, while down below in the square fronting the library thirty to forty fresh-faced students of both sexes formed a scrum and sang songs. Not once did they get to the end of a single song; the crackdown was always too rapid, too brutal for that. Whenever Eun-sook witnessed such a scene, always from a distance, it was a safe bet that she would have an unquiet night ahead of her. Even if she did manage to fall asleep, a nightmare would soon jerk her awake.

It was in June, after the first end-of-term exams, that her father suffered a cerebral hemorrhage, which left him paralyzed down his right side. Her mother got work as a pharmacy assistant, becoming the breadwinner of the family. Eun-sook took a leave of absence from university. During the day she looked after her father, then when her mother got home from work she headed out to her own part-time job, packaging and selling at a downtown bakery until they closed their doors at 10 p.m. She would be able to snatch a few scant hours of sleep before getting up with the sun and preparing packed lunches for her two younger siblings. She returned to university when the year's turning saw her father regain enough movement to be able to feed himself, but only managed a single term before she had to drop out again to earn the fees for the following term. After scraping through the second year in this on-off fashion, she finally gave up on the idea of graduating. When her professor recommended her for the publishing job, she took it.

For her mother this was all a source of regret, but she herself thought differently. Regardless of their financial situation, she knew she would never have been able to graduate. Rather, she would have ended up ineluctably drawn into that scrum of students. There, surrounded by those youthful faces, she would have held out for as long as possible. Being left as the sole survivor would have been the most frightening thing.

It wasn't as though she'd had her mind set solely on surviving.

After she went home that day and changed into a clean set of clothes, she'd slipped back out of the main gate without her mother knowing. Night was beginning to fall by the time she got back to the municipal gym. The entrance was closed and there was no one to be seen, so she went to the Provincial Office. The complaints department was also deserted. Aside, that is, from several rotting corpses, which were giving off a foul miasma. They looked just as they had when she and Seon-ju had handled them; perhaps the civilian militias hadn't had time to transfer them all to the gym, and these had been left behind.

In the lobby of the annex she finally found some other people. One of the university students she'd seen working in the cafeteria called out to tell her that the women were all supposed to go up to the first floor.

When Eun-sook went up the stairs and stepped into the small room at the end of the corridor, the women were in the midst of a heated debate.

"We have to be given guns, too. This fight needs everyone it can get."

"We'll only hand out guns to those who really want them. Who've resolved to see this through."

She spotted Seon-ju sitting at the end of the table, resting her chin in her hand. When Eun-sook went and sat down next to her, Seon-ju flashed her a quick smile. As ever, the latter was economical with her words, but when the debate came to a close she calmly announced that she was for the side that wanted guns.

It was around eleven o'clock at night when Jin-su knocked on the door. This was the first time any of them had seen him carrying a gun, and the sight was somewhat incongruous alongside the wireless radio he was never without.

"Could three of you stay here until the morning?" he asked. "We want to do some street broadcasts overnight, and three's all we need for that. The rest of you, please go home."

Of the three who stepped forward, each had been on the side that argued for the women to be given guns as well as the men.

Then the young woman from the cafeteria, the one who'd directed Eun-sook to the first floor, spoke up.

"We want to stay, too. We want to see this through together. That's why we came here, to be together."

Thinking back on it afterward, Eun-sook could never quite remember how Jin-su had managed to persuade them. Perhaps because she didn't want to. She could dimly recall something about how it would tarnish the reputation of the civilian militias if women were left behind in the Provincial Office to die with the men, but she couldn't be sure whether that argument had actually decided anything for her. She'd thought she'd come to terms with the idea of dying, yet something about death itself, the various forms it might take, still disturbed her. Having seen and handled so many dead, she'd imagined she would have become inured to it all, but on the contrary her fear had increased. She didn't want her last breath to be a gasp from a gaping mouth, didn't want translucent intestines spilling out through a gash torn into her body.

Seon-ju was one of the three women who had elected to stay behind. She took a carbine rifle for self-protection, listened to a brief explanation of how to use it, then slung it clumsily over her shoulder. Turning her back on the others without any good-byes, she followed the other two students down to the ground floor. Jin-su addressed the three women.

"You need to get as many people as you can to come out of their homes. As soon as the sun's up, the whole square in front of the Provincial Office has to be packed with demonstrators. We'll hold out until then, somehow or other, but by morning we'll need the support."

It was around 1 a.m. when the remaining women left the Provincial Office. Along with one other male student, Jin-su led them along the alleyway that fronted Nam-dong Catholic church. At the entrance to the alley, where the street lighting was sparse, he stopped.

"Now spread out. Each of you go and find a house to hide in, any house."

Had she ever had such a thing as a soul, that was the moment of its shattering. When Jin-su, rifle strap pressing against his sweat-soaked shirt, gave you all a farewell smile. But no, it had already shivered into fragments, when she'd come out of the Provincial Office and the sight of your diminutive frame, more like a child's than a teenage boy's, had stopped her in her tracks. Your pale blue tracksuit bottoms, your PE sweater—and then she'd seen the gun you were clutching. "Dong-ho," she'd called out, "why aren't you at home?" She marched up to the youth who was explaining to the others how to load a gun. "That kid is still in middle school. You have to send him home." The young man looked surprised. "He told me he was in the second year at high school; I had no reason not to believe him . . . we even sent the first-years home just now, but he never said anything." Eun-sook lowered her voice. "That's nonsense. Look at his face. And you're telling me he's in high school?"

The women waited until Jin-su disappeared around the corner before they began to break up. "Do you know anyone who lives around here?" the student who worked in the cafeteria asked her. She shook her head. "Come with me to Jeonnam Hospital, then. My cousin is a patient there."

At the hospital the lights in the lobby were all off and the entrance was locked. After the two of them had been banging on the door for a few minutes, a guard came out waving his flashlight at them. He was followed by the head nurse. The tension was evident in both their faces. They'd thought it was soldiers who'd come back.

The corridors and emergency stairs were as dark as the lobby. Guided only by the beam from the guard's flashlight, they eventually reached the ward where the other woman's cousin was staying. Here, the blackness was even more intense; sheets had been hung over the windows. Even in the pitch dark, they could sense that the patients and nurses were alert. The other woman left Eun-sook's side and went over to her aunt. "What are we going to do?" her aunt whispered. "They're saying that when the soldiers get here, the wounded will all be shot."

Eun-sook sat down beneath the window, her back against the wall.

"Don't sit near the window, it's dangerous." The speaker was a man who seemed to be the relative of the patient in the neighboring bed. It was too dark for Eun-sook to make out his face. "There was a lot of gunfire the day the soldiers retreated, too—

the clothes we'd hung over this window had bullet holes in them. If someone had been standing there, what d'you think would've happened to them?"

She shifted away from the window.

One of the patients was in critical condition, his breathing ragged; a nurse came to the ward every twenty minutes to check up on him. Every time the beam from her flashlight arced over the ward like a searchlight, the faces it illuminated were rigid with terror. *What are we going to do? Will the soldiers really come into a hospital? If they're saying the wounded will be shot, shouldn't we discharge them all as soon as it's light? It's barely been a day since your cousin recovered consciousness; what'll we do if the stitches tear?* To each of her aunt's whispered questions, the student who'd worked in the cafeteria made an even quieter reply. "I don't know, Aunty."

How much time had passed? Eun-sook heard a faint voice, clearly coming from some distance, and turned toward the window. The voice grew stronger: it was a woman, speaking into a megaphone, but not Seon-ju.

"Citizens, please join us in front of the Provincial Office. The army is reentering the city."

The silence swelled inside the room, like a huge balloon expanding to fill all corners. A truck rattled by in front of the hospital, and the voice grew even louder.

"We have resolved to fight to the end. Please come out and join us, fight with us side by side."

The voice dwindled, fading into the distance. Barely ten minutes had passed before the silence it had left in its wake was broken by the sound of soldiers. It was like nothing Eun-sook had ever heard before. The resolute, synchronized thud of a thousand pairs of combat boots. Tanks whose thunderous roar threatened to shatter paving slabs, shiver down walls like glass. She put her head between her knees. A small voice piped up from one of the ward beds. *Close the window, Mum. It's already closed. Close it tighter, then. Can't you close it tighter?* When the military din eventually swept past, the street broadcast could be heard once more. It cut through the silence muffling the heart of the city, faintly audible even from several blocks' distance. "Citizens of Gwangju, please join us in the streets. The army is coming."

When the unmistakable sound of gunfire was eventually heard, coming from the direction of the Provincial Office, Eun-sook was already wide awake. She could have pressed her hands over her ears, could have screwed her eyes tight shut, shook her head from side to side or moaned in distress. Instead, she simply remembered you, Dong-ho. How you darted away up the stairs when she'd tried to take you home. Your face frozen with terror, as though escaping this importunate plea was your only hope of survival. *Let's go together, Dong-ho. We ought to leave together, right away.* You stood there clinging to the second-floor railing, trembling. When she caught your gaze, Eun-sook saw your eyelids quiver. Because you were afraid. Because you wanted to live.

Slap Six

"How is he planning to get it past the censors?" the boss muttered. He was examining the invitation card that had just been delivered by a young man from Mr. Seo's theater. He almost appeared to be talking to himself, but Eun-sook knew that the question was aimed at her.

"Could he be rewriting the whole script from the beginning? But there's less than a fortnight left until the performance . . . how are they going to rehearse?"

The initial plan had been to publish the play this week and ensure that a review appeared in the newspapers' literary sections the week after. That would be a good way of publicizing the stage performance, which in turn would offer an opportunity to promote the book; they had also decided that, during the run, Yoon would sell copies of the play at the entrance to the theater. But now that the censors had made publication impossible, even performing a play based on that eviscerated script was off the table. And now, for whatever reason, Mr. Seo had gone and sent the invitation cards as though none of this had happened.

The door to the office banged open and Yoon staggered in, straining under the weight of a large box of books. His glasses were all misted up.

"Someone take my glasses off for me."

Eun-sook rushed over and removed his glasses. Panting, Yoon bent down and let the box thud to the floor by the table. Eun-sook opened it up with a Stanley knife and took out two copies. After handing one to the boss, she turned her attention to the cover. There, where she had been expecting the name of the fugitive translator, she discovered that of the boss's relative, the one who had emigrated to the United States. The whole office had been in a state of high tension after handing this book's proofs in to the censors—now, it transpired that it had been sent off to the printer's with only two paragraphs removed.

Eun-sook covered the tabletop with newspaper before helping Yoon to unload the books. Accompanied by a press release, each copy went into an envelope bearing the publisher's logo, and these were then stacked in neat piles to be distributed to the press the following morning.

"Looks good," the boss remarked, again as if to himself. He cleared his throat then spoke again, more formally. "It's come out really well."

He took off his reading glasses and stood up. Struggling with his coat, he tried and failed several times to get his right arm into the sleeve. His arthritic shoulder, stiff and painful at the best of times, always seemed to get worse during winter. Eun-sook stopped what she was doing and went to help him.

"Thank you, Miss Kim."

From close up, his open, unguarded eyes seemed unaccountably tinged with fear, and the lines circling his neck were deeper than one would have expected for someone his age. Eun-sook found herself wondering why someone so timid and feeble would maintain close relationships with writers who were under the scrutiny of the authorities, why he kept on publishing precisely those books that earned the censors' attention.

The boss had barely left the building before Yoon also clocked off for the day, leaving Eun-sook alone in the office.

Rather than go home early, she went and sat by the freshly printed books. Trying to recall the translator's face, she found that for some reason or other she was unable to remember his appearance in any detail. It no longer hurt to let her fingers skim over her bruised right cheek. Even pressing down produced a sensation that barely qualified as pain.

The book was a nonfiction treatise examining the psychology of crowds. The author hailed from the UK, and most of the examples she had selected were from modern European history. The French Revolution, the Spanish Civil War, the Second World War. The translator had himself elected not to include the chapter on the 1968 student movement, believing that it would only serve to jeopardize the rest of the book in the eyes of the censors. He'd still translated this chapter, though, for inclusion in a full and revised edition at some point in the future. In the introduction, he wrote,

> The decisive factor dominating the morality of the crowd has not yet been clearly identified. One point of interest is the emergence *in situ* of a particular ethical fluctuation separate from the moral standard of the individuals who constitute the crowd. Certain crowds do not blench at the prospect of looting, murder, and rape, while on the other hand, others display a level of courage and altruism which those making up that same crowd would have had difficulty in achieving as individuals. The author argues that, rather than this latter type of crowd being made up of especially noble individuals, that nobility which is a fundamental human attribute is able to manifest itself through borrowing strength from the crowd; also, similarly, that the former case is one in which humanity's essential barbarism is exacerbated not by the especially barbaric nature of any of the individuals involved, but through that magnification which occurs naturally in crowds.

The censors had scored through four lines in the paragraph following that one. *Bearing that in mind, the question which remains to us is this: what is humanity? What do we have to do to keep humanity as one thing and not another?* Eun-sook could remember the precise thickness of the line that had been drawn through these sentences. She could recall the translator's fleshy neck, his shabby navy sweater, his sallow complexion; his long, blackened fingernails constantly fumbling with the glass of water. But she still couldn't picture his face to herself with any precision.

She closed the book and waited. Turned to face the window, and waited for darkness to fall.

She had no faith in humanity. The look in someone's eyes, the beliefs they espoused, the eloquence with which they did so, were, she knew, no guarantee of anything. She knew that the only life left to her was one hemmed in by niggling doubts and cold questions.

The fountain had been dry that afternoon. Gun-toting soldiers were hauling fresh bodies over to the wall in front of the Provincial Office. They dragged them by the legs, so that the backs of their heads bumped and scraped against the ground, then tossed them next to the bodies that had already been dumped there. Some of the soldiers had had a bright idea for increasing the efficiency of this process: a small group was marching into the Provincial Office's inner yard, each holding a corner or edge of a huge waterproof tarp on which the corpses of a dozen people were being transported in one go. When Eun-sook had walked by, unable to prevent her eyes from widening at the sight, three soldiers rushed over and aimed their guns at her chest. *Where are you going? Just home. I've been visiting my aunt; she's not well.* Her voice had been cool and steady, but her upper lip trembled as she spoke.

She left the square on their orders, making an effort to regulate her steps. When she reached Daein Market, a huge tank came roaring down the main road. *They want to show everyone that it's all over,* she'd thought to herself, almost absentmindedly. *That all the protesters have been killed.*

The neighborhood where she lived with her parents, though close to the university district, was so utterly devoid of human life, it was as though a plague had ravaged it. When she rang the bell, her father instantly came running out, only unlocking the main gate for the brief time it took to usher her inside. He got her to hide up in the kitchen loft, then moved the tall cupboard over beneath the entrance so that it wouldn't attract anyone's notice. As morning wore into afternoon, the heavy tread of combat boots started to be heard. Sounds of doors being slid open, of struggling bodies being dragged, of something being smashed, sounds of begging and pleading. *No-oo, our kids weren't at the demo, they've never even touched a gun.* Someone pressed the bell for Eun-sook's house, and her father's voice rang out in answer. *Our daughter's still in high school. Our sons are in middle school and primary school, what would they be doing at a demo?*

When she finally came down from the loft the next evening, her mother informed her that the corpses had been loaded into the city garbage trucks and driven off to a mass grave. Not just those that had been dumped in front of the fountain; even the unidentified bodies, the ones that had been kept in coffins in the gymnasium—all had been taken away.

The government and municipal offices had reopened, as had the schools. The shops had their shutters back up and had resumed trading. Since martial law was still in effect, no one was permitted to be out in the streets after 7 p.m. Soldiers also set up checkpoints arbitrarily throughout the day, and anyone who had come out without their ID card was hauled off to the nearest police station.

In order to make up for the class time that had been missed, the majority of schools extended their summer term into early August. Until the day when they closed for the summer holidays, Eun-sook called the Provincial Office's Public Inquiry Department every single day, from the phone booth next to the bus stop. *It's not right for the fountain to be on, for God's sake make it stop.* The handset became sticky with the sweat from her palm. The staff at the department responded patiently, assuring her that the matter would be discussed. Once, Eun-sook's call was answered by a middle-aged woman, clearly sympathetic yet sadly resigned. *I'm sorry, but you need to stop calling. There's nothing we can do about the fountain. You sound like you're still in school, no? It's best you forget, then, and concentrate on your studies.*

Outside the window, a pale fluttering trembled the curtain of gathering dark.

It was time for her to get up and leave the office, but instead she remained where she was, unmoving. The flakes of snow silently sifting down looked as soft and white as freshly ground rice flour. Nevertheless, she could not think of them as beautiful. Today was supposed to be the day for her to forget the sixth slap, but her cheek had already healed. It barely even hurt anymore. When the next day dawned, then, there would be no need to forget the seventh slap. There would never be a day when she would forget the seventh slap.

Snowflakes

After the set change, the lights come up again slowly. In the center of the stage stands a tall woman in her thirties, her white hemp skirt recalling the kind of homespun item worn by mourners. When she silently turns to face the left-hand side of the stage, this appears to be the cue for a tall, slim man dressed in black to emerge from the wings. He comes walking toward her, carrying a life-sized skeleton on his back. His bare feet tread the boards with carefully measured steps, as though he fears he might slip in the empty air.

The woman turns now to the right, still silent as a marionette. This time the man who steps out from the wings is short and stocky, though in his black clothes and with the skeleton on his back he is identical to the first. The two men glide toward each other from their opposite sides, like images from some old-fashioned film, proceeding in slow motion as their projectionist laboriously cranks the handle. They reach the center of the stage at the same time, but they do not pause. Instead, they simply carry on to the other side, as though forbidden to acknowledge the other's presence.

There isn't a single empty seat in the house. The front rows look to be mainly made up of actors and journalists, perhaps because this is the opening night. When Eun-sook and the boss had been making their way to their seats and she'd glanced to the back of the auditorium, four men in particular had caught her eye. Though they were interspersed among the rest of the audience, she'd been in little doubt that they were plainclothes policemen. *What is Mr. Seo going to do?* she'd thought. *When those men hear the*

lines that the censors scored through coming out of the mouths of these ac-
tors, will they jump up from their seats and rush onto the stage? That chair
whirling through the air above the table in the university canteen,
the spurts of blood from the boy's forehead, the cooling plate of
curry. What would happen to the production crew, watching the
scene unfold from the lighting box? Would Mr. Seo be arrested?
Would he escape only to live a hunted existence, a fugitive whom
even his own family would struggle to track down?

Once the figures of the men have melted back into the wings,
their steps sliding forward with a dreamlike lassitude, the woman
begins to speak. Or so it seems. In actual fact, she cannot be said
to say anything at all. Her lips move, but no sound comes out. Yet
Eun-sook knows exactly what she is saying. She recognizes the
lines from the manuscript, where Mr. Seo had written them in
with a pen. The manuscript she'd typed up herself, and proofread
three times.

After you died I could not hold a funeral,
And so my life became a funeral.

The woman turns her back on the audience, and the lights
go up in the long aisle between the seats. Now a strapping man
is standing at the end of the aisle, his clothes of tattered hemp.
His breathing comes ragged as he walks toward the stage. Unlike
the aloof, impassive figures who glided across the stage mere moments ago, this man's face is contorted with feeling. He stretches
both arms up above his head, straining for who knows what. His

lips gupper like a fish on dry land. Again, Eun-sook can read what
those lips are saying, though speech is an uncertain name for the
high-pitched sound shrieking out from between them.

Oh, return to me.
Oh, return to me when I call your name.
Do not delay any longer. Return to me now.

After the initial wave of perplexity has swept through the audience, they subside into cowed silence and gaze with great concentration at the actor's lips. The lighting in the aisle begins to
dim. The woman on stage turns back to face the audience. Silent
as ever, she calmly watches the man walking down the aisle, in-
voking the spirits of the dead.

After you died I couldn't hold a funeral,
So these eyes that once beheld you became a shrine.
These ears that once heard your voice became a shrine.
These lungs that once inhaled your breath became a shrine.

Eyes wide open yet seeming not to see the waking world,
shrieking up into the empty air while the woman merely moves
her lips, the man in hemp mounts the stairs to the stage. His up-
raised arms swing down, grazing her shoulders as though brushing away snow.

The flowers that bloom in spring, the willows, the raindrops
*   and snowflakes became shrines.*
The mornings ushering in each day, the evenings that daily
*   darken, became shrines.*

The lighting over the seats comes back up, dazzling the audience. All of a sudden, Eun-sook sees a boy standing in the aisle. He is wearing a white tracksuit and gray sneakers, and clutching a small skeleton to his chest, hugging it to him as though he is cold. When the boy begins to walk toward the stage, a group of actors emerge from the darkness at the end of the aisle and follow on behind, stooped at ninety-degree angles and with their arms dangling down, looking like four-legged animals. There is something grotesque and supernatural about the sight of these men and women, around a dozen altogether, proceeding down the aisle with their black hair hanging. Mumbling, shrieking, moaning, they raise their heads, revealing lips that twitch incessantly. Every time these sounds grow louder, the boy turns to look behind him, flinching back at what he sees. This slows him down, so the group soon overtakes him and is first to reach the steps to the stage.

As Eun-sook stares transfixed at this scene unfolding, her own lips twitch without her knowing. As though in imitation of the actors, she calls out a silent name, the sound dying heavy in her throat. *Dong-ho.*

The young man at the back of the procession turns around, still bent double, and snatches the skeleton out of the boy's grasp. Passed from one dangling hand to another, the skeleton eventually reaches the old woman at the head of the procession, her back so bent that it resembles the letter ㄱ. Hanks of gray-streaked hair falling down around her face, she clasps the skeleton in a tight embrace as she mounts the steps to the stage. The woman in white and the man in hemp, who have been standing up there all the while, quietly move aside to let her pass.

Now the only moving figure is that of the old woman.

Her footsteps are so incredibly slow, they barely disturb the air around them, while an abrupt cough from the audience seems an intrusion from another world. As though this is the trigger, the boy starts out of his stasis, leaping up onto the stage in a single bound and pressing himself against the old woman's bent back. Like a child being given a piggyback, like the spirit of someone dead. So close, it's impossible to say whether or not they are touching.

Dong-ho.

Eun-sook bites down on her lip, hard, as multicolored streamers flutter down from the ceiling onto the stage. Scraps of silk on which funeral odes are written. The actors gathered in front of the stage abruptly straighten up. The old woman stops in her tracks. The boy, who had been inching along behind her, turns to face the audience.

Eun-sook closes her eyes. She does not want to see his face.

After you died I couldn't hold a funeral, so my life became a funeral.
After you were wrapped in a tarpaulin and carted away
   in a garbage truck.
After sparkling jets of water sprayed unforgivably from the fountain.
Everywhere the lights of the temple shrines are burning.
In the flowers that bloom in spring, in the snowflakes. In the
   evenings that draw each day to a close. Sparks from the
   candles, burning in empty drinks bottles.

Scalding tears burn from Eun-sook's open eyes, but she does not wipe them away. She glares fiercely at the boy's face, at the movement of his silenced lips.

4

The Prisoner, 1990

It was a perfectly ordinary pen, a black Monami Biro. They spread my fingers, twisted them one over the other, and jammed the pen between them.

This was the left hand, of course. Because I needed my right hand to write the report.

It was just about bearable, at first. But having that pen jammed into the exact same place every day soon rubbed the flesh raw, and a mess of blood and watery discharge oozed from the wound. Later on it got bad enough that you could actually see the bone, a gleam of white amid the filth. They gave me some cotton wool soaked in alcohol to press against it, but only then, only once the bone was showing through.

There were ninety other men in the cell with me, and more than half had that selfsame bit of cotton wool stuck there between their fingers. You weren't allowed to talk to each other. Your eyes would just flick down to that scrap of cotton wool then up to meet the other man's gaze, but only for a split second. That was enough to acknowledge the mark you shared. No need to linger.

I'd assumed they'd give the wound time to heal up once it had got into that state. I was wrong. I got to know a new pain instead, when the cotton wool was removed and the pen jammed back between the fingers, mashing that raw meat to a pulp.

There were five cells in total, laid out in a kind of fan shape. In the central area on the other side of the bars, the soldiers with their guns could keep watch over all five cells at the same time. When they first shoved us in and locked the doors behind us, not a single one of us dared to ask where they'd brought us. Even the kids from high school knew enough to keep their mouths shut. We stayed silent, avoided each other's eyes. We needed time to process what we'd experienced that morning. A scant hour's worth of silent despair, that was the last grace left to us as humans.

That black Monami Biro would be there on the table every time I went into the interrogation room. Lying in wait. The first stage in a sequence which unfolded exactly the same way every time, the whole process seemingly designed to hammer home a single fact: that my body was no longer my own. That my life had been taken entirely out of my hands, and the only thing I was permitted to do now was to experience pain. Pain so intense I felt sure I was going to lose my mind, so horrific that I literally did lose control of my body, pissing and shitting myself.

Once the sequence had been brought to its usual conclusion, the questions began. The voice that asked the questions was never anything other than calm and composed, but whatever answer I made would inevitably bring the same result: a rifle butt to the face. I couldn't fight the instinct that made me shrink back against the wall and shield my head with my arms, even though that only ever made things worse. When I fell down, they stamped on my back with their army boots. Only until I was just on the point of losing consciousness; then they would flip me over, and trample my shins instead.

Once you were told to leave the interrogation room and go back to your cell, you might be forgiven for thinking that you'd be able to relax, to let your guard down a bit. But that would be a mistake.

We had to sit on the floor of the cell for hours at a time, shoulders and back ramrod straight. Eyes front, too, directly at the window. The sergeant would bark out a warning if your gaze even threatened to stray from those iron bars, and one older guy actually had a cigarette stubbed out on his eyelids as an example to the rest of us. One of the high-school kids inadvertently scratched his neck, once; him, they beat until he lost consciousness and went as limp as a rag doll.

There were close to a hundred of us all told, wedged in so tight you could feel the knees of the guy behind you pressing into the small of your back. We sweated buckets; literally, it was like we'd been caught in a downpour. Our throats were screamingly dry, but we were only given water three times a day, with meals. I remember how savage, how animalistic that thirst was, how I would have jumped at the chance of literally anything to wet my lips, even a splash of urine would have done. And I remember the constant terror of thinking I might accidentally fall asleep. The terror of having a cigarette stubbed out on my eyelid, so vivid I could practically smell the singed flesh.

And the hunger, of course. How persistently it clung on, a

translucent sucker attached to the nape of the neck. I remember those moments when, hazy with exhaustion and hunger, it seemed as though that sucker was slowly feeding on my soul.

Three times a day, every day, the meal we were given was exactly the same: a handful of rice, half a bowl of soup, and a few shreds of kimchi. And this was shared between two. The relief I felt when I was partnered with Kim Jin-su says something about the state I'd been reduced to at that point, a brute animal with whatever had once been human having been gradually sucked out. Why was I so relieved? Because he looked like he wouldn't eat much. Because he was pale, with dark shadows around his eyes that made him look like he belonged in a hospital. Because of his empty, life-less eyes.

A month ago, when I saw his obituary, those eyes were the first things I thought of. Those eyes that used to track my every movement as I fished out a bean sprout from the watery soup; that regarded me in silence as I stared with open hatred at any morsel of food that passed his lips, consumed with the fear that he might take it all for himself; those cold, empty eyes, utterly devoid of anything that could be said to resemble humanity. Just like my own.

There's something I still haven't been able to figure out.

Given that I was partnered with Kim Jin-su and ate the exact same meals as him every single day, how come he died and I'm still living?

Was it that he suffered more than me?

No, it wasn't that. I bore more than my fair share of suffering.

Was it that he got less sleep than me?

But sleep is still every bit as elusive for me as it was for him. Even now, there's not a single night where I'm able to snatch more than a few hours of shallow rest, rest that barely deserves the name. And it'll be like that for as long as this life clings to me.

When you first called me to ask about Kim Jin-su, professor, it made me wonder. Even after I'd arranged to meet you, after you called again, I was still wondering. Every day without exception, those same questions niggled away at me: why did he die, while I'm still alive?

Do you remember, professor, that first time we spoke, when you told me that Kim Jin-su was "by no means an isolated case"? According to you, it was more than likely that many of us former prisoners would end up taking our own lives.

I suppose you thought you were helping me? Trying to save my life from heading down that same sorry track? Yes, I can well imagine that those were the kind of noble ideas you had in mind. But when it came to it, this dissertation you were planning to write, was it really going to benefit anyone other than yourself?

You explained about the "psychological autopsy" you wanted to conduct on Kim Jin-su, but I still couldn't understand it. You wanted to record my testimony—what for? Would that bring Jin-su back to life? Our experiences might have been similar, but they were far from identical. What good could an autopsy possibly do? How could we ever hope to understand what he went through, he himself, alone? What he'd kept locked away inside himself for all those years.

• • •

It's true that Jin-su did suffer some unusually brutal torture, even compared with the rest of us. Perhaps because there was something strangely delicate about him. Almost feminine. And somehow that rubbed the guards the wrong way.

But I only heard these stories at least a decade after the fact. At the time, I had no idea.

What I heard was that the soldiers made him get his penis out and rest it on the table, threatening to cane it with a wooden ruler. Apparently, they made him strip and took him out to the patch of grass in front of the guardhouse, where they tied his arms behind his back and made him lie down on his stomach. The ants nibbled at his genitals for three hours.

I heard that after he was released, he had nightmares about insects almost every single night.

As for what he was like before then, I can't help you. I only ever saw him from a distance, you see, striding down the corridors of the Provincial Office.

In 1980, when it happened, he was still only a freshman at university. The hair on his upper lip was little more than a scrubby patch of fluff, and he had these thick, dark lashes that stood out against his pale skin. Every time I saw him he seemed to be in a great hurry, his skinny arms swinging back and forth by his sides.

I know the kinds of things he was busy with, at least: dealing with the wounded, organizing the treatment of the corpses, obtaining coffins and flags, arranging the funeral ceremonies . . . all that sort of thing.

You know, I really wouldn't have predicted he'd stay behind on the last night. There were only the hardliners left at that point, and they were mainly workers. Most of the students, on the other hand, had called for the Provincial Office to be evacuated before the army reentered the city, insisting that no more lives be needlessly thrown away. They left their own guns in the lobby and went home to their beds; I would have had Jin-su down for one of them. Even when I saw him there, I had my doubts. I wouldn't have been surprised if he'd snuck away before midnight.

Twelve of us, including Jin-su and myself, formed one group. We gathered in the small conference room and made the usual introductions, though I'm pretty sure none of us imagined that our acquaintance would last beyond that night. We each made a cursory will, jotted down our names and addresses, and slipped these into our shirt pockets, so we'd be easy to identify. All these things we were making contingency plans for, which were almost upon us, the strange thing is that they still didn't actually seem real. At least, not until we heard over the wireless that the army had reentered the city. We all tensed up then.

Around midnight, the militia chief called Jin-su out into the corridor and told him to get the women out of the building. This guy had such a voice on him, even those of us inside the conference room could hear every word he said. At the time, I guessed that the reason the chief had picked Jin-su to see the women to safety was because he'd decided our chances of holding out were hardly going to be affected by the absence of this fragile-looking young man. I remember watching Jin-su shouldering his gun and marching out of the room, his lips pressed into a thin line. *That's right*, I remember thinking, *if I were you, I'd find somewhere safe to hole up, and not worry about rushing back.*

So I was surprised, then, when he did come back. In the twenty-odd minutes since I'd last seen him the tension had completely drained from his face, but now he could barely keep his eyes open. He went straight over to the window, curled up on the faux-leather sofa, and promptly fell asleep. When I went over and shook him awake he didn't even open his eyes, just mumbled about how he was sorry, but he was tired, just so tired.

Strangely enough, his exhaustion seemed to infect the rest of us, sapping our energy, and one by one everyone ended up sitting on the floor, slumped against the nearest wall. Even I wasn't immune—I couldn't keep myself from curling up next to Jin-su on the sofa. How to explain it? It was precisely the time when we should have been one hundred percent alert, and instead we allowed ourselves to succumb to drowsiness, sleep blanketing our eyes and ears.

Somehow, the sound of the door being cautiously inched open made it through the fog of unconsciousness, and I opened my eyes to see some kid slipping into the room—a middle-schooler, I could tell by his cropped hair. He crept over to the sofa and sat down with his back against it.

"Who are you?" My voice was hoarse with sleep. "Who are you, and where have you come from?" He'd shut his eyes tight as soon as he sat down, and he kept them shut when he answered me.

"I'm so tired. I'm just going to sleep for a minute or two, here with Jin-su."

Jin-su had been sleeping like the dead, but that voice startled him awake.

"Dong-ho?" he demanded in a muffled whisper, seizing hold of the boy's arm. "Didn't I tell you to go home? Didn't you promise you would?" His voice was getting louder. "What the hell were you planning on doing here? You know how to fire a gun, do you?"

"Don't be angry, Jin-su," the boy ventured. There was a rustling sound, as those woken by the argument got stiffly to their feet.

"You'll surrender at the first opportunity," Jin-su insisted, still not letting go of the boy's arm. "Surrender, have you got that? Go out with your hands up. There's no way they'll harm a kid with his hands up."

In 1980 I was twenty-two, and I'd just gone back to university after completing my military service. I was planning on getting a job as a primary school teacher after I graduated, and maybe that was why they chose me to be our militia's leader that night—because I was a little bit older and had a steady head on my shoulders. For the most part, those who'd stayed behind in the Provincial Office were an unruly lot, and there wasn't much in the way of discipline going around. More like a mob than an organized militia.

The majority were still in their teens. There was even one kid, who went to evening classes after his job, who just wouldn't be convinced that, even if he loaded his gun and pulled the trigger, a bullet would actually come out. He went out to the yard and fired off a round into the night sky. Those of school age were the ones who balked at being sent home. They were so stubborn, they needed a lengthy talking-to before they were persuaded to leave.

The militia chief insisted on running through our "tactics" with me, though the plan turned out to be so flimsy it barely warranted such a description. The army was predicted to arrive at the Provincial Office at around 2 a.m., so we started filing out into the corridor at half past one. One of the adults was stationed at each window, while the younger boys lay on their stomachs in the spaces in between, ready to take over if the person next to them got shot. I had no way of knowing what tasks the other teams had been assigned, or whether our overall strategy had any realistic chance of success. The chief kept emphasizing that our aim was only to hold out until dawn, when hundreds of thousands of Gwangju's citizens would stream out into the streets and mass around the fountain.

It sounds foolish now, but at the time we half-believed those words. We knew there was a chance we might die, yes, but privately we thought we'd be okay. We were anticipating defeat, but also, and at the same time, thinking that we might somehow manage to come through after all. This wasn't just me; for most of us, especially the younger ones, our hopes outweighed our fears. We had no idea that, only the day before, a spokesman for our student militia had met with foreign journalists and announced that our defeat was certain. He'd told them that we all knew we were going to die, but that we weren't afraid of death. Such noble conviction, transcending all fear; but it's only the plain truth to say that this isn't how it was for me.

As for Kim Jin-su's thoughts on the matter, there's no way for me to tell. When he chose to come back after seeing the women to safety, was he fully expecting this decision to result in his death? Or was he more like me, erring on the side of optimism—thinking that death was far from inevitable, that we would manage to hold the Provincial Office after all, then be able to live the rest of our lives free from shame?

• • •

It wasn't as though we didn't know how overwhelmingly the army outnumbered us. But the strange thing was, it didn't matter. Ever since the uprising began, I'd felt something coursing through me, as overwhelming as any army.

Conscience.

Conscience, the most terrifying thing in the world.

The day I stood shoulder to shoulder with hundreds of thousands of my fellow civilians, staring down the barrels of the soldiers' guns, the day the bodies of those first two slaughtered were placed in a handcart and pushed at the head of the column, I was startled to discover an absence inside myself: the absence of fear. I remember feeling that it was all right to die; I felt the blood of a hundred thousand hearts surging together into one enormous artery, fresh and clean . . . the sublime enormity of a single heart, pulsing blood through that vessel and into my own. I dared to feel a part of it.

At one o'clock in the afternoon, while the speaker in front of the Provincial Office was playing the national anthem, the soldiers opened fire. I'd been standing in the middle of the column of the demonstrators, but when the bullets came flying, I turned and ran. That sublime feeling that I'd been tapping into, that enormous heart I'd felt briefly a part of, was smashed to pieces, strewn over the ground as so much rubbish. And the gunfire wasn't only in the square; snipers were also positioned on the roofs of the surrounding buildings. Beside me and in front of me people crumpled to the ground, but I kept on running. Only when I was sure I'd left the square far behind did I let myself stagger to a stop. I was so out of breath, I genuinely thought my lungs would burst. My face a mask of sweat and tears, I sank to my knees on the steps leading up to a shop door. Its shutters were down. A small group had gathered in the street, and I heard them talking about raiding the police stations and reserves barracks to get guns. They were clearly made of much sterner stuff than I was. *We're sitting ducks like this. They'll gun us down, the lot of us. Paratroopers even broke into the houses in my area. I was so scared I slept with a kitchen knife by my pillow. Shooting hundreds of rounds like that in broad daylight—I'm telling you, the world's gone mad!*

One of them jogged off to fetch his truck, and I stayed there slumped on the steps until he drove back. I thought about whether I really had it in me to carry a gun, to point it at a living person and pull the trigger.

It was already late at night by the time the truck I was riding in returned to the center. We'd twice taken a wrong turn, and when we'd got to the barracks, we'd found that the guns had already been looted, so it turned out to be a wasted trip. In the meantime, I had no way of knowing how many had fallen in the street fighting. All I remember is the entrance to the hospital the following morning, the seemingly never-ending line of people queuing up to give blood; the doctors and nurses striding through the blasted streets, white gowns bloodstained, hands gripping stretchers; the women who handed up stale rice balls, water, and strawberries to the truck I was riding in; the strains of the national anthem, and "Arirang," which everyone was singing at the top of their voice. Those snapshot moments, when it seemed we'd all performed the miracle of stepping outside the shell of our own selves, one person's tender skin coming into grazed contact with another, felt as though they were rethreading the sinews of that world heart, patching up the fissures from which blood had flowed, making it beat again. That was what captured me, what has stayed with me ever since. Have you even known it, professor—that terrifying intensity, that feeling as if you yourself have undergone some kind of alchemy, been puri- fied, made wholly virtuous? The brilliance of that moment, the dazzling purity of conscience.

It's possible that the kids who stayed behind at the Provin- cial Office that day experienced something similar. Perhaps they would have considered even death a fair exchange for that jewel of conscience. But no such certainty is possible now. Kids crouching beneath the windows, fumbling with their guns and complaining that they were hungry, asking if it was okay for them to quickly run back and fetch the sponge cake and Fanta they'd left in the conference room; what could they possibly have known about death that would have enabled them to make such a choice?

When the announcement came over the wireless that the army would reach the Provincial Office within the next ten minutes, Jin-su propped his gun against the wall, stood up, and said, "It's possible that we could hold out until the morning and run the risk of dying in the process, but that's not an option for the youngsters here." For all the world as though he himself were a seasoned adult of thirty or forty, rather than a boy barely out of school. "We have no choice but to surrender. If death seems the only other outcome, put down your guns and surrender right away. Look for a way to live."

I don't want to talk about what happened next.

There is no one now who has the right to ask me to remember any more, and that includes you, professor.

No, none of us fired our guns.

None of us killed anybody.

Even when the soldiers stormed up the stairs and emerged toward us out of the darkness, none of our group fired their guns. It was impossible for them to pull the trigger knowing that a person would die if they did so. They were children. We had handed out guns to children. Guns they were not capable of firing.

I found out later that the army had been provided with eight hundred thousand rounds that day. This was at a time when the population of the city stood at four hundred thousand. In other words, they had been given the means to drive a bullet into the body of every person in the city twice over. I genuinely believe that, if something had come up, the commanding officers would have issued the order for the troops on the ground to do just that. If we'd all done as the student representatives said, piled our guns in the lobby of the Provincial Office and attempted a clean surrender, we would have run the risk of the soldiers turning those same weapons on unarmed civilians. Every time I recall the blood that flowed in the small hours of that night—literally flowed, gushing over the stairs in the pitch dark—it strikes me that those deaths did not belong solely to those who died. Rather, they were a substitute for the deaths of others. Many thousands of deaths, many thousands of hearts' worth of blood.

Out of the corner of my eye I could see blood silently seeping from people I'd been speaking with mere moments before. Unable to tell who had died and who survived, I lay prone in the corridor, my face pressed into the floor. I felt someone write on my back with a magic marker. *Violent element. Possession of firearms.* That was what someone else informed me was written there, afterward, when they threw us into the cells at the military academy.

• • •

Those who hadn't been carrying a gun at the time of their arrest were classified as mere accomplices, and were released in batches up until June, leaving only the so-called violent elements, those who had been caught in possession of firearms, still in the military academy. That was when the program of torture entered a different phase. Rather than brutal beatings, our captors now chose more elaborate methods of inflicting pain, methods that would not be too physically taxing for them. "Hairpin torture," where both arms were tied behind the back and a large piece of wood inserted between the bound wrists and the small of the back; waterboarding; electric torture; the method known as the "roast chicken," which involved trussing the victim with ropes and suspending them from the ceiling, where they were then beaten while being spun around. Before, they'd tortured us in order to extract the particulars of actual crimes. Now, all they wanted was a false confession, so that our names could be slotted neatly into the script they had already devised.

Kim Jin-su and I continued to receive a single tray and share its scant meal between us. It took an enormous feat of will to put what we'd experienced a few hours ago in the interrogation room behind us and wield our spoons in stony silence, fighting the temptation to scrap like animals over a grain of rice, a shred of kimchi. There was one man who knocked his meal tray over and screamed, *I can't take any more of this! What's going to happen to me if you shovel the whole lot down yourself?* As he grappled with his partner, a boy pushed between them and stuttered, *D-don't do that.* I was taken aback; this was the first time I'd ever seen that quiet, shy-seeming kid open his mouth.

W-we were r-ready to die, you know.

It was then that Kim Jin-su's empty gaze rose to meet mine.

At that moment, I realized what all this was for. The words that this torture and starvation were intended to elicit. *We will make you realize how ridiculous it was, the lot of you waving the national flag and singing the national anthem. We will prove to you that you are nothing but filthy stinking bodies. That you are no better than the carcasses of starving animals.*

The boy with the stutter was called Yeong-chae. It was a name Kim Jin-su pronounced frequently in the afternoons following that initial altercation. In the ten or so minutes after the meal, which was when the guard tended to relax his vigilance, he would address the boy in a soft, friendly tone. *You must be hungry, Yeong-chae, no? Kim Yeong-chae, where's your family from? I'm a Gimhae Kim, too. Which branch? You're fifteen, right, well then, no need for honorifics with me. I'm only four years older than you at the most. I don't look my age, do I? Oh, well, all right. Call me uncle, then. We're distant relatives, after all.*

From listening in to their conversation, I learned that the boy hadn't continued his education beyond middle school, and was learning carpentry at his uncle's woodworking shop. He'd joined the civilian militia to follow in the footsteps of this uncle's son, who was two years older; this cousin, to whom he'd always looked up, had been killed that final night at the YMCA. *I-I l-like to eat sp-sponge cake the best. W-with S-sprite.* Yeong-chae's eyes stayed dry while he told the story of his dead cousin, but when Jin-su asked him what his favorite food was, he had to scrub at them with his fists. With his right fist, that is. His left remained in his lap. I stared

at it, at the cotton wool poking out from between those clenched
fingers.

I was constantly racking my brain.

Because I wanted to understand.

Somehow or other, I needed to make sense of what I'd experienced.

Watery discharge and sticky pus, foul saliva, blood, tears and
snot, piss and shit that soiled your pants. That was all that was
left to me. No, that was what I myself had been reduced to. I was
nothing but the sum of those parts. The lump of rotting meat
from which they oozed was the only "me" there was.

Even now I find summer difficult to endure. When runnels of
sweat trickle down over my chest and back, itching like the bite of
insect mouths, that time when I was nothing but a lump of meat is
suddenly back with me, the feeling unchanged, and I have to take
a deep, steady breath. Grind my teeth together, and take another
deep, steady breath.

When a square wooden cudgel is squeezed in between my shoulder blades, manipulated so that my screaming joints are forced
as far apart as the physical composition of my body will possibly
allow, when this body writhes and contorts and the words spew
from its lips, *for God's sake, stop, I did wrong,* seconds strung together
with jerked, juddering gasps, when they insert a drill bit beneath
my fingernails and toenails, shuddered-in breath spat out in a rush,
for God's sake stop, I did wrong, seconds patched with broken groans,

rising into a wail, *make this body disappear, please, for God's sake, just wipe it off the face of the earth.*

From that first summer into the autumn, during the time when we were made to write our evidence reports, a single-story building was erected on the grounds of the barracks. It was intended to function as a military law court, so they could pass sentence without the hassle of transferring us anywhere else. In the third week of October, when a cold snap set in, the trial was convened. At that point it had been ten days since we'd completed our reports. Those ten days were the first torture-free period of our confinement. The wounds patterning our bodies slowly began to heal, dark red scabs forming over them.

I remember that the trial lasted for five days, with two sessions per day. Around thirty people were sentenced during each session. There were so many defendants, we filled the rows of benches all the way to the back. Spaced among us at regular intervals, the soldiers kept their hands resting on their guns.

"All bow."

I bowed my head at the staff sergeant's command.

"Bow lower."

I bowed lower.

"The chief justice will be here any moment now. If there's so much as a squeak from any of you, you'll be shot in your seat, got it? You just keep your heads down and your mouths shut until it's over. Understand?"

They stalked between the benches with their rifles loaded and primed, and anyone whom they judged to be slumping got a butt to the back of the head. From outside the court building, the grasshoppers' shrill cries reminded us that the seasons had turned. The blue prison uniforms we were wearing had been handed out that morning, and still gave off the smell of detergent. As I held myself rigid I mulled over those words, "you'll be shot in your seat." I held my breath as though I really was expecting to be executed at any moment. At the time, death seemed as though it would be something refreshing, like slipping on that clean new uniform. If life was the summer that had just gone by, if life was a body sullied with sweat and bloody pus, clotted seconds that refused to pass, if life was a mouthful of sour bean sprouts that only served to intensify the hunger pangs, then perhaps death would be like a clean brushstroke, erasing all such things in a single sweep.

"The chief justice is present."

It was then that my ears picked up a strange sound, coming from in front of me. I'd been bowing so low my chin was almost touching my chest, but that sound made me raise my head an inch, just enough so I could scan the rows in front. Someone was singing, though the sound was more like a stifled whimper. It was the opening bars of the national anthem. By the time I realized that the singer was young Yeong-chae, other voices had joined in for the chorus. Almost in spite of myself, my own voice was drawn out of my throat. We who had had our heads bowed as though we were already dead, who had been sitting there as nothing but loose agglomerates of sweat and blood, were for some reason permitted to continue our quiet song unchecked. The soldiers didn't scream at us, didn't drive their rifle butts into our heads, didn't shove us up against the wall and shoot us as they'd threatened to do. We were left to bring the song to its close, the silence between each bar a perilous window of calm within the cool air of the summary court, laced with the grasshoppers' chirping.

I received a nine-year sentence, and Kim Jin-su was given seven years.

Of course, those terms were meaningless. The military authorities continued to release us in batches, even those who'd been sentenced to capital punishment or life imprisonment, up until Christmas the following year. These releases were always officially justified as taking place "on amnesty." It was almost a tacit acknowledgment of the absurdity of the charges.

Two years after we were released, as the year was drawing to a close, I saw Kim Jin-su again. It was late at night, as I was making my unsteady way home after a lengthy session downing beers with an old classmate from middle school. I saw a young man sitting in a shabby roadside shack, hunched over a bowl of hangover soup, and it stopped me in my tracks. That posture was so painfully familiar; the head bowed over the soupy rice, the spoon clenched tightly, to be wielded with the kind of diligence that kids reserve for their homework. Empty eyes framed by long, thick lashes, peering into the bottom of the soup as though its oily swirls of black oxblood were congealing to form a riddle, one whose answer would remain impenetrable.

When I entered the shack and sat down across from Kim Jin-su, the gaze he regarded me with was cold and dispassionate. Feeling the onset of a hangover, I smiled and waited for him to show that he forgave my intoxication. For the ghost of a smile to appear on his face, the smile of one who has just surfaced from sleep.

As we each inquired how the other had been, something like transparent feelers reached tentatively out from our eyes, confirming the shadows held by the other's face, the track marks of suffering that no amount of forced jollity could paper over. Neither of us had managed to go back to university, and we were both still living at home, a burden to our families. Jin-su worked at his brother-in-law's electric goods shop; I'd held down a position at my relative's restaurant for a short while, but had quit some time ago. I told him I was thinking of waiting until New Year and then joining a taxi company, maybe even saving up to get my own taxi at some point. He made no response.

"My brother-in-law advised me to do something similar," he said flatly. "He said I ought to study for an HGV license. After all, it's not like an office job is an option. But how am I going to get a driving license? These days even simple sums are enough to make my head hurt. Some days it's a struggle just to tally up the payments in the shop. The most basic addition. The headaches are so bad, it's impossible for me to memorize anything for an exam."

I told him that I frequently suffered from a toothache that didn't seem to have any physical cause, that there weren't many days when I didn't have to take painkillers.

"Can you sleep?" he asked listlessly. "I can't. That's why I'm here chasing my hangover. I had two bottles of soju before this. My sister doesn't like me to drink at home, you see. I mean, not that she gets angry or anything. She just cries. But then that only makes me want another drink." He looked up from his soup. "How about a glass now? Just the one?"

We stayed there drinking until the streets began to fill again, with men and women hastening to work, the collars of their woolen coats turned up against the cold. We poured glass after glass of strong, clear alcohol in the vain hope that this would help us forget. My memory of that night is a series of jump cuts, which later collapsed completely. I can't remember when we parted or how I managed to make it home. The only shards that have lodged themselves in my brain are the sensation of cold liquid dripping onto my corduroy trousers when Jin-su knocked over the bottle; the sight of him clumsily trying to blot the spillage with the sleeve of his sweater; the moment when he could no longer hold his neck up, and had to rest his forehead on the table.

Afterward, we continued to meet up now and then and drink through the night. Seven years dragged by in this way, with each of us seeing in the other a crooked mirror image of our own pathetic lives: failing to gain any qualifications; being involved in a car accident; getting into debt; suffering injury or illness; meeting kind-hearted women who made us dare to believe that our suffering was finally over, only to see it all turn to shit through no one's fault but our own, and eventually end up alone again. Burdened by nightmares and insomnia, numbed by painkillers and sleeping pills, we were no longer young. There was no longer anyone who would worry over us or shed tears over our pitiful lot. We even despised ourselves. The interrogation room of that summer was knitted into our muscle memory, lodged inside our bodies. With that black Monami Biro. That pale gleam of exposed bone. That familiar, broken cadence of whimpered, desperate pleas.

At some point during those seven years, Jin-su said to me, "There used to be people I was determined to kill." His deep black eyes, not yet entirely clouded by intoxication, watched me intently. "I thought that, whenever my time came to die, I would take those people with me." Wordlessly, I filled his glass. "But I don't have those thoughts anymore. I'm worn out." *Hyeong*, he called me. Brother. But instead of raising his eyes to meet mine, he kept his head bowed over the glass of clear alcohol, as though any words I might speak would be found there. "We carried guns, didn't we?" This didn't seem to merit a response. "We thought they would defend us, didn't we?" Jin-su smiled faintly down at his glass, as though used to answering his own questions. "But we couldn't even fire them."

Last September, I bumped into him late at night when I was heading home after my taxi shift. One of those drizzling autumn days. I'd just turned a corner and there, from beneath the rim of my umbrella, I saw Kim Jin-su waiting for me. He had the hood of his black waterproof jacket up over his head. Perhaps because I was so startled, I remember being gripped by an odd rage, wanting to punch that ghost-pale face. Or no, not punch it, just rub my hands over its contours and erase the expression I saw there.

Not that his expression was hostile, you understand.

He looked exhausted, of course, but that was hardly anything out of the ordinary. I'd barely ever seen him looking otherwise that past decade. But there was something else in the planes and shadows of his face that night, something different. Some inexplicable emotion that was not quite resignation, not quite sadness or even malice, was visible beneath those long lashes. Part submerged, like ice in water.

I ushered him through the darkened streets to my house. He never said a word the whole way.

"What's the matter?" I asked him once we were home and I could change out of my wet clothes. He pulled his raincoat off over his head, folded it, and put it on the floor by the mattress.

Then he sat down next to it, ramrod straight in a thin cotton T-shirt. His posture made me recall the barracks, and that unaccountable anger welled back up in me. Ever so slightly hunched, the sight was identical to the one I'd seen every single day that summer nine years before. The stink of his sweat was rank in my nostrils. As he sat there looking up at me, his dark face seemed a nauseating mixture of submission, resignation, and blankness.

"I can't even smell any booze on you; how long were you waiting for? And in this rain." Eventually, he opened his mouth.

"There was a trial yesterday."

"A trial?" I repeated.

"You remember Kim Yeong-chae? He was in the cell with us." I sat down facing Jin-su. At first, I sat up straight as though imitating him, but I quickly realized what I was doing and lolled back against the chilly wall. "The stutterer. My distant relation."

"Yeah, I remember." For some reason, I didn't want to hear whatever Jin-su was going to say next.

"He's ended up in the psychiatric hospital this time."

"Right." I got to my feet and went to have a look in the fridge. The shelves were practically bare, but four bottles of soju were lined up in the salad drawer. Two days' worth of emergency medicine.

"He'll probably never get out."

I pulled out two bottles and stood them on a tray with a pair of shot glasses. I gripped the bottles by the necks to remove the lids; cold droplets of condensation made my palms slick.

"They say he almost killed someone."

I scooped some stir-fried anchovies out of a Tupperware container and onto a plate, then some beans boiled in soy sauce. It was all I had. I suddenly had the idea of putting the soju in the freezer compartment. What would it feel like to crunch on cubes of frozen soju, to hear them crack against my teeth?

"There's not much in the way of snacks." I set the tray down by the mattress, but Jin-su didn't so much as glance at it. Instead, he carried on talking, his words gradually speeding up.

"The public defender said Yeong-chae had slit his own wrists six times in the past ten years. That he had to take sleeping pills and get drunk every night just so he could get to sleep."

I filled Jin-su's glass. With any luck I'd be able to get away with just a single shot, then I could spread out the quilt, lie down, and try to get some sleep. I'd tell him he could carry on drinking for as long as he wanted, and go home whenever the rain let up. I didn't let myself wonder about how often Jin-su had met up with that kid in the nine years since we'd shared a cell, or how the latter had been living in the meantime. Whatever Jin-su had come here to say, I didn't want to hear it.

The dawn's faint light was beginning to leach into the sky, but the rain was still mizzling down and outside the window it was as dark as evening. Eventually, I spread the quilt over the mattress and lay down.

"Get some shut-eye," I told him curtly. "You look like you haven't slept in about a year."

He filled his own glass and tossed it back. While I tossed and turned in my sleep, the quilt pulled up to my face, he carried on talking at me. A slurred stream of high-flown words and random babble. It was no good to me.

Looking at that boy's life, Jin-su said, *what is this thing we call a soul? Just some nonexistent idea? Or something that might as well not exist?*

Or no, is it like a kind of glass?

Glass is transparent, right? And fragile. That's the fundamental nature of glass. And that's why objects that are made of glass have to be handled with care. After all, if they end up smashed or cracked or chipped, then they're good for nothing, right, you just have to chuck them away.

Before, we used to have a kind of glass that couldn't be broken. A truth so hard and clear it might as well have been made of glass. So when you think about it, it was only when we were shattered that we proved we had souls. That what we really were was humans made of glass.

That was the last time I saw Kim Jin-su alive.

I saw his obituary in the paper that same year. I had no idea what had happened to him in the meantime, during those three months that had seen autumn give way to winter. He did leave a message at the taxi office once, but we weren't allowed to make personal calls during work hours, and when I called him back after my shift was over, he didn't pick up.

There'd been an unusually large amount of rain that autumn, and every time the rain did stop the temperature immediately plummeted. Whenever I found myself heading home after a night shift, I would automatically slow down before rounding that corner. Even now that I know for a fact he's dead, I still do exactly the same thing. Whenever I pass that corner, and particularly when it's raining, I can see him in my mind's eye standing there, his face pale as a ghost's against the night's dark. His black raincoat.

His funeral was a neat and proper affair. I recognized his deep double eyelids and long lashes in the faces of his family, and even that same blankness to the eyes, hinting at unknowable depths.

His sister, who had clearly been stunningly beautiful at one time and who still retained a haggard loveliness even now, gave me a perfunctory handshake and then turned immediately away. They didn't have enough coffin bearers so I volunteered and accompanied the family to the crematorium. I only stayed until I saw the coffin enter the oven, though. On the way home, I remember there was no bus that would take me all the way into the center, so I got off at the three-way junction and walked for the final thirty minutes.

I never got a look at the suicide note.

And did they really find this photo next to it?

He never talked to me about it, not one word.

Of course, he and I were close in some senses, but think about it; how close could we really have been? Yes, we relied on each other, but we also wanted to smash each other's face in. To erase each other's very existence. To thrust each other permanently out of sight.

And you want me to explain this photo, professor?

But how? Where to even begin?

The people in the photo are dead, they've been shot, their blood is all over the ground. It's in the yard in front of the Provincial Office. One of the foreign journalists must have taken the photo. No Korean reporters were allowed in, you see.

Ah, I know what must have happened—he must have found it in some photo collection and clipped it out. There were plenty of those collections circulating at the time; you must have seen one yourself, no?

And now you want me to guess why Kim Jin-su kept this photo with him until the very end, why it was found with his suicide note?

You want me to tell you about these dead kids, professor? Like felled trees, lying in such an unnaturally straight line.

What right do you have to demand that of me?

We kept our faces pressed into the corridor carpet for as long as the soldiers ordered us to. Around dawn, they hauled us to our feet and took us down to the yard. They made us kneel in a line, our backs to the walls, with our hands tied behind us. An officer came over. He'd worked himself up into quite a state. His combat boots thudded into our backs, driving our heads down into the dirt, while he spat out a string of curses. "I was in Vietnam, you sons of bitches. I killed thirty of those Vietcong bastards with my own two hands. Filthy fucking Reds." Kim Jin-su was kneeling next to me. The officer stamped on his back, grinding his face into the gravel. When he let him back up, I saw slender threads of blood clinging to Jin-su's forehead.

That was when five of the younger boys came down from the second floor, holding their hands above their heads. Four of them were high-school students. When the army first began to pepper the building with indiscriminate machine-gun fire, lit by flares as bright as the noonday sun, I'd ordered them to hide in the conference room's cupboard. The fifth was Dong-ho, the middle-schooler who'd had that brief argument with Kim Jin-su. They'd waited until the sound of gunfire could no longer be heard, then put down their weapons and come out to surrender. All as Jin-su had told them to do.

"Look at these bastards!" the officer yelled. He was practically frothing at the mouth. "Want to surrender, do you, you fucking Reds? Want to save your precious skins?" With one foot still up on Kim Jin-su's back, he raised his M16, took aim, and fired. The bullets tore into those school kids without hesitation. My head inadvertently jerked up, and when he whooped in the direction of his subordinates, "As good as a fucking movie, right?" I saw how straight and white his teeth were.

Now do you understand? The kids in this photo aren't lying side by side because their corpses were lined up like that after they were killed. It's because they were walking in a line. They were walking in a straight line, with both arms in the air, just like we'd told them to.

Some memories never heal. Rather than fading with the passage of time, those memories become the only things that are left behind when all else is abraded. The world darkens, like electric bulbs going out one by one. I am aware that I am not a safe person.

Is it true that human beings are fundamentally cruel? Is the experience of cruelty the only thing we share as a species? Is the dignity that we cling to nothing but self-delusion, masking from ourselves this single truth: that each one of us is capable of being reduced to an insect, a ravening beast, a lump of meat? To be degraded, damaged, slaughtered—is this the essential fate of humankind, one that history has confirmed as inevitable?

I once met someone who was a paratrooper during the Busan uprising. He told me his story after hearing my own. He said that they'd been ordered to suppress the civilians with as much violence as possible, and those who committed especially brutal actions were awarded hundreds of thousands of won by their superiors. One of his company had said, "What's the problem? They give you money and tell you to beat someone up, then why wouldn't you?"

I heard a story about one of the Korean army platoons that fought in Vietnam. How they forced the women, children, and elderly of one particular village into the main hall, and then burned it to the ground. Some of those who came to slaughter us did so with the memory of those previous times, when committing such actions in wartime had won them a handsome reward. It happened in Gwangju just as it did on Jeju Island, in Kwantung and Nanjing, in Bosnia, and all across the American continent when it was still known as the New World, with such a uniform brutality it's as though it is imprinted in our genetic code.

I never let myself forget that every single person I meet is a member of this human race. And that includes you, professor, listening to this testimony. As it includes myself.

Every day I examine the scar on my hand. This place where the bone was once exposed, where a milky discharge seeped from a festering wound. Every time I come across an ordinary Monami Biro, the breath catches in my throat. I wait for time to wash me away like muddy water. I wait for death to come and wash me clean, to release me from the memory of those other, squalid deaths, which haunt my days and nights.

I'm fighting, alone, every day. I fight with the hell that I survived. I fight with the fact of my own humanity. I fight with the idea that death is the only way of escaping this fact.

So tell me, professor, what answers do you have for me? You, a human being just like me.

5

The Factory Girl, 2002

You Remember

She told you that the moon was called "the eye of the night."

You were seventeen when you first heard it described that way. It was a Sunday night in spring, when your small labor union group had gathered at Seong-hee's house. She lived on the top floor, so after the meeting was over you all went up onto the roof, sat in a circle on sheets of newspaper, and ate peaches. Seong-hee was twenty, and her romantic nature was frequently fed by poetry. *It seems that way, doesn't it?* she said, gazing up at the full moon. An eye cold and pale as ice, looking down on you from the center of the black sky. *That the moon is the eye of the night.* You were the youngest of the group, and for some reason those words scared you. *It makes it seem frightening when you call it that, Seong-hee.* At that, everyone burst out laughing. *I've never known such a scaredy-cat!* one of the women giggled, popping a slice of peach into your mouth. *What's so scary about the moon?*

Now

You get out a cigarette and put it between your lips. You light it, take a deep drag, and feel your tense throat muscles ache.

You're alone in the second-floor office, a room little bigger than twenty *pyeong*. None of the windows are open. The heat and humidity of an August evening pummels you as you sit there in front of your computer. You've just deleted two spam e-mails. You still haven't clicked on the latest arrival in your in-box.

Your hair is cropped short. You are wearing jeans and ultra-marine sneakers. The sleeves of your pale gray shirt are just long enough to cover your elbows, and at the top of your back the sweat-soaked fabric has darkened to an inky black. In spite of your androgynous outfit, your small frame and slender neck make you seem delicate, almost fragile.

The sweat clinging to the hair behind your ears crawls down over your jaw and drips onto your shirt collar. You run a finger along your upper lip, wiping away the beads of moisture, and click on the e-mail. You read it slowly, twice, then close the browser and switch off the computer. As the monitor's blue glow fades, the last light in the darkened room, you draw repeatedly on your cigarette, exhaling the smoke in a steady stream.

The cigarette is only half smoked when you place it in the ashtray and stand up. You stick your sweat-gummed fists into the pockets of your jeans. As you walk over to the window, the air inside the sealed office is stiflingly close. The distance from your desk to the window seems a vast expanse. Your movements are sluggish, like wading through water, and even this minimal effort leaves your entire body slick with sweat. Glittering droplets bead your cropped hair.

You stand in front of the window and rest your forehead against the dark glass. The only reflection it holds is that of your own image. The glass is slightly damp, and refreshingly chilly. You gaze down at the dark, deserted alleyways, dotted with ashen streetlights. You stand up straight, turn to look at the clock on the opposite wall, then, as if doubting its accuracy, check its time against your watch.

Up Rising

I was listening to that sound.

The sound woke me up, but I didn't have the courage to open my eyes, so I kept them closed and strained to listen in the darkness.

Footsteps, so quiet as to be almost imperceptible. Two feet marking time with the lightest of treads, like a child learning a new and difficult dance.

I felt a knot of pain tightening in my solar plexus.
I couldn't tell whether it was fear I was experiencing, or happiness.
Eventually, I got up.
I walked toward the sound, and stopped in front of the door.
The wet towel that I'd hung on the handle to try and get a bit of moisture into the air; a pale swatch in the darkness.

That was the source of the sound.
Drops of water steadily tapping down, blotted by the papered floor.

Now

You place the Dictaphone in front of you on the desk, next to three small, blank cassette tapes, each with a white label attached. Your face shiny with sweat, your breathing, despite your wide-open eyes, as deep and regular as someone asleep, you regard them.

Ten years ago, when Yoon first contacted you, you were still working at the labor rights organization run by Seong-hee. It was only after getting in touch with her that Yoon had managed to obtain your contact details. You'd listened in silence as he explained the topic of his current dissertation and mentioned the name of the specific civilian militia that he'd chosen as the focus for his "psychological autopsy."

"I'll think about it and give you a call."

When you called him back an hour later and turned down his request for an interview, Yoon simply said that he understood. The following spring, he sent you a copy of his dissertation. You didn't read it.

A few days ago, contacting you again for the first time in ten years, he said that he really wanted to meet you, just once. His words and tone were cautious. Even a phone interview, he said, would do.

"The dissertation I sent you back then, did you get round to reading it?"

"No."

He seemed somewhat thrown by this, but quickly regained his composure. He told you that he'd since made further inquiries regarding the ten members of the militia whom he'd interviewed for the dissertation, and discovered that there are now only eight left; two had taken their own lives. Of the remaining eight, seven agreed to a follow-up interview. He had taped these interviews, and was planning to include the transcripts in the conclusion of the book he was currently writing, a book in which the dissertation he wrote ten years previously will form a single chapter.

After finishing his speech, he paused.

"Are you listening?"

"Yes, I'm listening."

Whenever you take a phone call, you habitually make a note of any numbers that come up in the course of the conversation. On the memo pad next to you were the digits 10, 8, 2, 7.

"There were several women who were taken into custody at the time, but I've had trouble tracking down an appropriate witness. Even in cases where they were willing to provide a testimony, it was too brief, too simple. Anything painful was just skimmed over . . . please, do me this favor. I need you, Lim Seon-ju, to be the eighth witness for this book."

This time you didn't ask for time to think about it.

"I'm sorry, but I can't help you." Your voice betrayed no emotion.

A few days later, though, Yoon sent a parcel to the office. Inside were the tape recorder and blank tapes that you are looking at now, and a letter. His handwriting was such a scrawl that it was difficult to make out the words, but you struggled through to the end. *I understand that you'd prefer not to meet me in person, but might you be able to record your testimony instead and send the tapes to me?* His business card was attached to the bottom of the letter with a paper clip.

You reseal the letter to make it look as though it has never been opened, and put it into your locker. The dissertation is still there, from when you filed it away all those years ago; you take it out and peruse it with care, reading through each of the transcripts included in the appendix. Twice. Once your colleagues have all gone out to lunch, the office is quiet. Before they return, you put the dissertation back exactly where you found it and close the locker securely, as though wanting to hide from yourself the fact that you've read it.

Up Rising

How strange.

Only the sound of dripping water; yet I remember it as though someone really did come to my door.

That winter night, it seemed as though those imagined footsteps that caused a knot of pain inside me were the stuff of waking reality, while the damp floor and the dripping towel were the substance of a dream.

Now

You insert the cassette into the Dictaphone.

Your name will be kept anonymous, Yoon had written. Any names of people or places that might enable someone reading to identify you will be assigned a randomly chosen initial. Recording your testimony this way, not only do you get to avoid a face-to-face meeting, but what's particularly convenient is that you can erase any parts you want to, whenever you like, and rerecord them until you're happy.

Still, you don't press down on the "record" button. Instead, you run your fingers carefully over the smooth plastic corners of the device, as though checking for a flaw in the design.

By coincidence, voice recordings are precisely what you deal with in this office, every day.

Your job is to transcribe the recordings of informal gatherings and forums, to categorize photographs of certain events, along with reports, trials, and testimonies—anything relating to environmental issues—and file them in the record room. For events of particular importance, you produce three or four versions from the original camcorder film, edited depending on what the footage might later be used for. These exercises are time-consuming and monotonous, and not especially distinguished. They are tasks that require you to spend the majority of your time alone. Your workload is, of course, heavier than that of your colleagues, but this isn't a problem for you; you're used to working evenings and weekends. Rather than being given a monthly salary, you get paid per job. The amount you're able to earn this way doesn't even cover basic living costs, but the financial situation was even worse at the labor organization.

Over the ten years you've been working at your current job, the killings that you spend your days archiving have all been slow and drawn out. Radioactive elements with long half-lives. Additives that either needed to be banned or had been banned already but were still being used illegally. Toxic industrial waste, agricultural chemicals, and fertilizers that cause leukemia and other cancers. Engineering practices that destroy the ecosystem.

The tape recordings that Yoon has in his possession will deal with a different world altogether.

You imagine the office of this man whose face you have never seen. You imagine the tapes that will be lined up on his shelves. Each with a name and date, scrawled on its white label in his sloppy handwriting. You imagine the deaths that will be imprinted along the tape's smooth, brown belt, the living voices that will speak them: a world of guns, bayonets, and cudgels; sweat, blood, and flesh; wet towels, drill bits, and lengths of iron piping. Nothing slow about such deaths.

You put the Dictaphone back down on the desk, bend over, and open your locker. You pull Yoon's dissertation out and turn to the page where the first transcript begins.

They made us keep our heads bowed the whole time, so we had no idea which direction the truck was heading.

We could tell when we were going uphill though, and when the truck eventually stopped and they dragged us out we'd clearly come a fair way out of the city. There was a building, but I couldn't tell what kind of building it was. Then they started with the "disciplinary beatings"—you know, like they do in the army, only far worse. Kicking us, swearing at us, hitting us with the butts of their rifles. I remember one of us, a plump man in his forties, snapped and started yelling. "Just kill me and have done with it!"

That really did it. The soldiers rushed over to him and started wielding their cudgels in earnest. They beat him so viciously it really did look like they weren't going to stop until they'd killed him. He seemed to go from thrashing around to completely limp in a single moment. Even his feet had stopped twitching. They splashed a bucket of water over his face and took a photograph. The blood was dripping from his face. Blood and water. The rest of us just held our breath.

That wasn't the only time something like that happened. We spent three days there, in the main hall inside that building. It didn't seem like an army place, just an ordinary hall like you'd find in any public building. The soldiers mostly went away during the day, just a couple stayed behind to guard us. I assumed they went back into the city center to crack down on any remaining demonstrators. In the evenings they were drunk by the time they got back to us. Then there'd be another round of disciplinary beatings, and woe betide anyone who did anything other than cower in absolute silence. Anyone who lost consciousness would get kicked into a corner, then the soldier would grab them by the hair and pound their head against the wall. Once they actually stopped breathing, the soldiers would splash water over their face and take a photo, then order them to be stretchered away.

I prayed every night. I don't mean anything formal; I'd never been a regular at any temple or church. I just asked to be set free from that hell. But they were answered, you see, my prayers were answered. There were around two hundred of us being held captive there, and after three days they released half of us. Including me. At the time we had no idea what was going on, but later on I found out that the army had been about to make a strategic retreat to the suburbs and they thought too many prisoners would just get in the way. They'd chosen who was going to be released purely at random. So it was just blind luck.

We were told to keep our heads down when the truck took us back down the hill, too. But, you know, I was quite young at the time, and I suppose curiosity just got the better of me. I was kneeling right at the very edge of the truck, so if I twisted my neck I could get a look outside through the gap in the sideboards.

I . . . . I'd never dreamed that they'd been keeping us in the university.

The building where we'd been kept was the new lecture hall, just behind the sports ground where me and my friends had used to play football at the weekends. Now, with the army occupying the campus, there were no other signs of human life. The truck itself was rattling along, but otherwise the road was silent as the grave. Then I saw them, lying on a patch of grass by the side of the road. They just looked like they were asleep, at first. Two students in jeans and college sweaters, with a yellow banner laid across their chests as if they'd both been holding up an end. The letters had been done in thick Magic Marker, so I could read it even from inside the truck. END MARTIAL LAW.

It's really extraordinary how those young women, their faces, ended up scored into my memory so deeply, you know? I mean, I only caught just a fleeting glimpse of them.

But now, each time I fall asleep, and each time I wake up again, I see those faces. Their pale skin, their closed mouths, their legs stretched out straight . . . it's so clear, so vivid, it's like they're really there. Just like the face of the man with blood dripping from his jaw, his eyes half closed . . . etched into the insides of my eyelids. Inside, where I can't get at it. Where I'll never be able to scrape it off.

Your own dreams are filled with sights that are quite different from the ones haunting this first witness.

At the time, you were more closely acquainted than most with brutalized corpses, yet there have only been a handful of times in the past twenty-odd years when your dreams have been vivid with blood. Rather, your nightmares tend to be cold, silent affairs. Scenes from which the blood has dried without a trace, and the bones have weathered into ash.

The streetlamp's feeble glow encases it in a lead-gray aureole, but beyond the reach of its light the night is pitch black. It isn't safe to stray beyond the bounds of this lit place. You do not know what might be lurking in the darkness. But you'll be all right as long as you don't move a muscle. You don't venture outside the circle of light. You merely wait, stiff with tension. Wait for the sun to rise and the outer dark to dissipate. You've held out this far, you mustn't waver now. Safer to keep your feet absolutely still, rather than risk taking a false step.

When you open your eyes, it's still dark. You get up from your bed and switch on the bedside lamp. This year you will turn forty-two, and there has been only one single period in your entire adult life during which you lived with a man. And you didn't even manage a year at that. Living alone means there's no need to consider whether you'll be waking another person up, so you walk straight over to the door and switch on the light. You switch on all the lights, in the bathroom, the kitchen, the entrance hall, and fill a glass with cold water, your hand trembling only very slightly, and drink.

Now

You rise from your seat at the unmistakable sound of someone turning the door handle. You bend down, slide the dissertation back into the locker, and call out "Who is it?"

You've locked the door.

"It's Park Yeong-ho."

You walk over to the door, turn the key in the lock, and open it.

"Working at this hour?" you both chorus, and then, as if on cue, burst out laughing.

Team leader Park affects nonchalance as he peers over your shoulder into the office. Traces of laughter still linger around his mouth, but you can see the suspicion in his eyes. His thick-set frame is tending toward a paunch, his fringe an attempt to mask a receding hairline.

"It's because we've got the Kori meeting tomorrow, of course. There're still a few documents missing." Park drops his bag by his desk and switches on his computer. He carries on justifying his presence, like someone who has dropped by another's house un-announced. "Something's come up that means I'll have to head down to the plant myself. Anyhow, I'll need every file we have if I'm going to convince them to finally shut down the reactor. I was really surprised when I saw the lights on," he continues, his voice now excessively genial. "Naturally, I'd assumed the place would be empty." Suddenly he pauses and glances around, looking faintly disconcerted. "What's with the heat?" He strides over to the wall and flings the windows wide open, then switches on both fans. He walks back to his desk, shaking his head in bewilderment. "You thinking of renting the place out as a sauna?"

You are the oldest of the employees here. Your juniors are extremely reserved around you, possibly slightly intimidated by the way you keep to yourself, diligently getting on with your allotted tasks. They address you using the honorific *seonsaeng*, but you respond with equally polite language, maintaining a respectful distance. When there's something they can't find, it's you they'll come to. "I'm looking for the documentation from such-and-such a forum in such-and-such a year; I've had a look in the records room but there's only some loose papers. Isn't there an official booklet containing all the speeches?" You search your memory, then explain: "That particular forum was only arranged at the last minute, so there wasn't time for a booklet to be produced. The speeches were recorded and then later transcribed, but those transcripts only exist as loose copies. Nothing was ever officially written down." Now and then, team leader Park likes to joke: "You're a human search engine, Miss Lim."

Now Park is standing in the middle of the office, waiting for his documents to print. His sharp eyes scrutinize the contents of your desk. A wad of damp tissue balled up in the ashtray, several cigarette butts, a mug of coffee. The Dictaphone and tapes.

He starts speaking the instant you intercept his probing gaze, as though conscious of the need to excuse himself.

"You seem to genuinely enjoy your work, Miss Lim. I mean, I look at you and I think, that's me in twenty years' time, if I keep on with this line of work . . ."

You understand that he is thinking of the meager pay, the laborious, irregular duties that are never sufficiently recompensed, your bony hands with their protruding veins running along the backs. Park is silent for a short while, and there is only the low, impatient whir of the laser printer as it spits out sheets of paper.

"We're all curious about you, Miss Lim," he resumes, his jovial tone even more pronounced than before. "We hardly ever get an opportunity to talk to you . . . you never have dinner with us after work, and you never let any of us know what you're thinking."

Park staples the printed sheets together and returns to his desk. He doesn't sit down, just fiddles with the computer mouse and then goes back to wait by the printer.

"I heard you were involved with the labor movement before you came here. Something to do with industrial accidents, wasn't it? And in the same organization as Kim Seong-hee, no less. I heard the two of you are quite close."

"Not exactly close," you answer, conscious of a friendship you can no longer claim. "But she was a great help to me. For a long time."

"I'm a different generation, so Kim Seong-hee's the stuff of legend to me. The late 1970s, the last days of the Yushin system and all President Park's emergency measures—I was raised on those stories. I remembering hearing about that Easter Mass on Yeouido, when Kim Seong-hee leaped up onto the podium, got hold of the CBS mic they were using for the live broadcast, and chanted 'We are human beings, guarantee labor rights' before she and the rest of her group were dragged away. A bunch of factory girls barely into their twenties. You were there too, weren't you, Miss Lim?"

Park's voice is part awed, part earnest. You shake your head.

"I didn't have anything to do with that. I wasn't in Seoul at the time."

"Oh, I see . . . it's just that I'd heard you spent some time in prison, and I'd always assumed it was because of that. So did the rest of our colleagues."

The moisture-laden wind is billowing in through the dark window. It strikes you as uncannily like a long inhalation. As though the night is itself some enormous organism, opening its mouth and exhaling a clammy breath. Then breathing back in, the stuffy air trapped inside the office being sucked into black lungs.

Overwhelmed with exhaustion, you bow your head. You spend a few moments peering at the brackish dregs at the bottom of your mug. You raise your head and smile in the way you always do when you cannot think of an appropriate reply. A delicate tracery of wrinkles fans out from the corners of your mouth.

Up Rising

You're not like me, Seong-hee.

You believe in a divine being, and in this thing we call humanity.

You never did manage to win me over.

I could never believe in the existence of a being who watches over us with consummate love.

I couldn't even make it through the Lord's Prayer without the words drying up in my throat.

Forgive us our trespasses, as we forgive those who trespass against us.

I forgive no one, and no one forgives me.

Now

The sign for the bus stop sheds its dim light down on you.

In your backpack is a notebook, pen and pencil, toiletries, a 250-ml bottle of water, the Dictaphone, and tapes.

The stop is a little out of the way, but all Line 3 buses come here. A succession of these buses have pulled up and whisked away their new passengers, and now you are alone. You stare silently at the paving slabs that lie beyond the reach of the lamp's light.

You turn and walk away from the sign. The straps of your backpack are cutting into your shoulders, so you slide your hands beneath them. The summer night is sultry, its hot fug of air dragging on your limbs. You pace a few yards one way, then turn and double back. Up to the edge of the road, then back.

When Park got his things together to leave the office, you shouldered your backpack and accompanied him out. The two of you walked to the bus stop together, your conversation meandering aimlessly and then trailing off when Park's bus arrived. He got on, found a seat, and nodded awkwardly in your direction in lieu of a formal good-bye. You nodded back.

What might you have been able to bring yourself to do if he hadn't shown up and interrupted you?

You wonder.

Would you have been able to summon the courage to press the "record" button?

Would you have been able to string together a continuous thread of words, silences, coughs, and hesitations, its warp and weft somehow containing all that you wanted to say?

You'd allowed yourself to believe that yes, you could have done all this; that was why you'd come into the office today, the public holiday for National Liberation Day. You'd even decided to stay up all night if that was what it took, hence the toiletries.

But would you really have gone through with it, even if you hadn't been interrupted?

If you go back now to your cramped, stifling room, will you be able to place the Dictaphone on the table in front of you and start again, from the beginning?

Last Monday, as soon as you heard the news about Seong-hee, you called her. You waited an hour before calling again, and on the fourth try the call finally went through. The first conversation you'd had in ten years was brief and matter-of-fact. You held your breath and strained to listen to the voice made hoarse from radiation therapy.

"It's been a long time," she rasped.

"I was wondering how you've been getting on."

You didn't offer to come and visit her in the hospital, so there was no need for her to protest about that. It was pure coincidence that the parcel from Yoon arrived at your office the very next day, yet now these two events seem inextricably entangled, taut as a barbed wire knot. The two of them together are almost more than you can bear.

Making the recording, and seeing Seong-hee.
The recording you need to make before seeing Seong-hee.

Enduring things is what you do best. Gritting your teeth and bearing them.

You still had a year of middle school left when you dropped out to get a job. Aside from the two years you spent in prison, you've never been out of work. You have been unfailingly diligent and unfailingly taciturn. Work is a guarantee of solitude. Living a solitary life; you are able to let the regular rhythm of long hours of work followed by brief rest carry you through the days, with no time to fear the outer dark beyond the circle of light.

You Remember

The work you did as a teenager, though, was different.

Those were fifteen-hour days with only two days off per month. "Weekends" were nonexistent. The wages were half of what the men got paid for the same work, and there was no overtime pay. You took pills to keep you awake, but exhaustion still battered you like a wave. The swelling of your calves and feet as morning wore into afternoon. The guards who insisted on body-searching the female workers every night before they went home. Those hands, which used to linger when they touched your bra. The shame. Hacking coughs. Nosebleeds. Headaches. Clumps of what looked like black threads in the phlegm you hacked up.

We are noble.

That was one of Seong-hee's favorite sayings. Every Sunday off work she spent attending lectures on labor law at the offices

of the Cheonggye Clothing Labor Union, and everything she heard there went into the notes she then used for your meetings. You had no particular apprehensions when you started attending those meetings, given that all Seong-hee said about them was that they were for studying *hanja*. And technically this was true; you and the other women really did study *hanja* each time you met. *We have to know 1,800 characters if we want to read a newspaper properly.* The first task of the evening involved you each writing thirty characters into your notebooks, memorizing them as you did so. Then Seong-hee would begin her labor lecture. *And that means . . . we are noble.* Seong-hee wasn't a natural orator, and whenever she lost her train of thought or couldn't quite recall the word she'd wanted she would use that phrase as a kind of stopgap. *According to the constitution, we are noble. As noble as anyone else. And just like anyone else, we have rights. According to labor law.* Her gentle, resonant voice almost put you in mind of a primary school teacher. *Jeon Tae-il died for the sake of this law.*

The labor union voted against the company-dominated union by a large majority. On the day the strikebreakers and policemen came to arrest its leading members, the hundreds of factory girls who were on their way from their dormitories to the second shift of the day formed a human wall. The oldest were twenty-one or twenty-two; most were still in their teens. There were no proper chants or slogans. *Don't arrest us. You mustn't arrest us.* Strikebreakers charged toward the shouting girls, wielding square wooden clubs. There must have been around a hundred policemen, heavily armed with helmets and shields. Lightweight combat vehicles whose every window was covered with wire mesh. The thought flashed through your mind: *What do they need all that for? We can't fight, we don't have any weapons.*

"Take off your clothes," Seong-hee bellowed. "All of us together, let's all take off our clothes." It was impossible to say who was first to respond to this rallying cry, but within moments hundreds of young women were waving their blouses and skirts in the air, shouting "Don't arrest us!" Everyone held the naked bodies of virginal girls to be something precious, almost sacred, and so the factory girls believed that the men would never violate their privacy by laying hands on them now, young girls standing there in their bras and pants. But the men dragged them down to the dirt floor. Gravel scraped bare flesh, drawing blood. Hair became tangled, underwear torn. *You mustn't, you mustn't arrest us.* Between these ear-splitting cries, the sound of square cudgels slamming into unprotected bodies, of men bundling girls into riot vans.

You were eighteen at the time. Dodging a pair of grasping hands, you slipped and fell onto the gravel, grazing your knees. A plainclothes policeman stopped in his wild dash forward just long enough to stamp on your stomach and kick you in the side. Lying with your face in the dirt, the girls' voices seemed to swing between yells and whispers as you drifted in and out of consciousness. You had to be carried to the emergency room of the nearest hospital and treated for an intestinal rupture. You lay there in the hospital bed, listening to the reports come in. After you were discharged you could have resumed the fight, stood shoulder to shoulder with your sisters. Instead, you went back down south to your parents' home near Gwangju. Once your body had had enough time to heal, you went back up to Incheon and got a job at another textiles factory, but you were laid off within a week. Your name had been put on the blacklist. Your two years' experience working in a textiles factory was now worth nothing, and one of your relatives had to pull some strings to get you a job as a machinist at a Gwangju dressmaker's. The pay was even worse than when you'd been a factory girl, but every time you thought of quitting you recalled Seong-hee's voice: *And that means . . . we are noble.* You wrote to her, calling her *onni*, older sister. *I'm getting on fine,* onni. *But it looks like it'll be a while before I can learn how to be a proper machinist. It's not so much that it's a tricky technique to learn, just that I'm not being taught very well. All the same, I have to have patience, right?*

For words like "technique" and "patience," you made the effort to write the *hanja* rather than just relying on the phonetic *hangeul* alphabet. You took time over the individual strokes of these characters that you'd learned at the meetings at Seong-hee's house. The replies, when they did come, were invariably brief: *Yes, that's right. I'm sure you'll do well in whatever job.* This lasted for around a year or two, and then the letters gradually fizzled out.

It took you three years to finally become a machinist. That autumn, when you were twenty-one, a factory girl even younger than you died at a sit-in at the opposition party's headquarters. The government's official report stated that she had cut her own wrists with the shards from a bottle of Sprite and jumped from the third floor. You didn't believe a word of it. Like piecing together a puzzle, you had to peer closely at the photographs that were carried in the government-controlled papers, to read between the lines of the editorials, which condemned the uprising in incensed, strident tones.

You never forgot the face of the plainclothes policeman who

had stamped on you. You never forgot that the government actively trained and supported the strikebreakers, that at the peak of this pyramid of violence stood President Park Chung-hee himself, an army general who had seized power through a military coup. You understood the meaning of emergency measure no. 9, which severely penalized not only calls to repeal the Yushin constitution but practically any criticism of the government, and of the slogan shouted by the scrum of students at the main entrance to the university. You pieced together the newspapers' oblique strands of misinformation in order to make sense of the subsequent incidents that occurred in Busan and Masan. You were convinced that those smashed phone booths and burnt-out police boxes, the angry mobs hurling stones, formed a pattern. Blanked-out sentences that you had to fill with your imagination.

When President Park was assassinated that October, you asked yourself: Now the peak has been lopped off, will the whole pyramid of violence collapse? Will it no longer be possible to arrest screaming, naked factory girls? Will it no longer be permissible to stamp on them and burst their intestines? Through the newspapers, you witnessed the seemingly inexorable rise of Chun Doo-hwan, the young general who had been the former president's favorite. You could practically see him in your mind's eye, riding into Seoul on a tank as in a Roman triumph, swiftly appropriating the highest position in the central government. Goose bumps rose on your arms and neck. *Frightening things are going to happen.* The middle-aged tailor used to tease you: "You're cozying up with that newspaper like it's your new beau, Miss Lim. What a thing it is to be young, and be able to read such fine print without glasses."

And you saw that bus.

It was a balmy spring day, and the owner of the dressmaker's had taken his son, a university student, to stay with relatives in Yeongam. Finding yourself with an unexpected free day on your hands, you were strolling the streets when you spotted it, an ordinary bus on its way into the city center. END MARTIAL LAW. GUARANTEE LABOR RIGHTS. Yellow Magic Marker screamed out from the white banners that hung out of the bus's windows. The bus was packed with dozens of girls from the textile factories out in the provincial towns, in their uniforms. Their pale faces put you in mind of mushrooms, which had never seen the sun, and they had their arms thrust out of the windows, banging sticks against the body of the bus as they sang. Their voices carried clearly all the way to where you had stopped in your tracks, and you remember them now as seeming to issue from the throat of some kind of bird.

We are fighters for justice, we are, we are
We live together and die together, we do, we do
We would rather die on our feet than live on our knees
We are fighters for justice

Every syllable so distinct in your memory. Entranced by that song, you stumbled blindly in the direction the bus had taken. A great throng of people had taken to the streets and were heading in the direction of the main square, in front of the Provincial Office. The students, who had been massing in front of their university's main gate since early spring, were nowhere to be seen. Those filling the streets were the elderly; children of primary school age; factory workers in their uniforms; young office workers, the men wearing ties, the women in skirt suits and high heels; middle-aged men wearing sweaters emblazoned with the logo of the "new village" movement, brandishing long umbrellas as though intending to use them as weapons. At the very front of this snaking column of people, the corpses of two youths who had been gunned down at the station were being pushed, in a handcart, toward the square.

Now

You climb the narrow stairs and emerge from the underground station. The refreshingly chill blasts of the train's air-conditioning had briefly dried the sweat on your skin, but now the humid air recongeals on your exposed flesh. It is a sweltering, tropical night. Though it's now close to midnight, the wind is still heavy with heat.

You stop in front of the information board by the hospital's entrance. Sliding your hands beneath the straps of your backpack, you quickly scan the timetable for the shuttle bus, see that it only runs during the day. Inhaling a lungful of lukewarm air, you turn away and begin to walk up the hill. Every now and then you wriggle a hand free and wipe away the sticky sweat that has trickled down from your neck.

Someone has spray-painted some crude graffiti on a shop's lowered shutter. Some guys are lounging under a parasol in front of a twenty-four-hour convenience store, knocking back cans of beer. You look up at the main building of the university hospital, which stands at the very top of the hill. You hear the girls' song carrying down across the years, from that bus in a past made hazy by time, all the way through to this night. *We would rather die on our feet than live on our knees. Let's join together for a minute's silence in tribute to those who have already paid the price, let's follow in their footsteps and fight to the end, because . . . because we are noble.*

• • •

You pass through the main gate into the hospital complex, heading along the path that stretches all the way up to the main building, first branching off to the annex and funeral hall. Its soft contours are lined by streetlights on both sides. Wreaths are lined up at the entrance to the funeral hall. Near them, young men are silently applying themselves to their cigarettes, yellow armbands over their white shirts.

It's late, but you are wide awake. The backpack is cutting into your shoulders and your back is drenched with sweat, but you don't care. You keep on walking, remembered dreams lancing through your mind.

You plummet from the roof of a high-rise building, clad in a suit of armor linked with hundreds of iron scales. Even though your brains are dashed out against the ground, you don't die. You pick yourself up, climb all the way back up the emergency stairs, walk straight over to the edge of the roof, and tip yourself off. Still you don't die, and it's back up the stairs to fall one more time. One layer of the dream unpeels, and you're sufficiently aware of the situation to wonder: *What good is a suit of armor if I'm falling from such a great height?* You haven't woken yourself up, though, merely passed through into another layer. You feel the weight of an enormous glacier bearing down on your body. You wish that you were able to flow beneath it, to become fluid, whether seawater, oil, or lava, and shuck off these rigid, impermeable outlines, which encase you like a coffin. Only that way might you find some form of release. Now this layer, too, unseams itself and collapses softly around you, exposing the dream's ultimate core. You are standing in the streetlamp's cone of ashen light, looking out into the gathering dark.

The dream grows less cruel as you move closer to wakefulness. Sleep grows thin, becomes brittle as writing paper, and eventually crumbles away. In the quiet corners of your conscious mind, memories are waiting. What they call forth cannot strictly be called nightmares.

You Remember

And you've succeeded, haven't you? Succeeded in putting it all behind you, in pushing away anyone who, with their insistence on raking up the past, threatened to cause you even the slightest pain.

You remember gritting out through clenched teeth, "What right do you have to tell my story to other people?" You remember Seong-hee's calm voice asking whether it would really be so difficult for you to make your story public. Not even ten years have proved sufficient for you to forgive her for that, for how serene she'd looked as she neatly dissected all the ways in which you'd failed. *If it had been me, I wouldn't have hidden away. I wouldn't have let the rest of my life slide by, too busy watching my own back.*

You remember the meek voice of the man who had been your husband for eight months. *You're quite pretty, even with your small eyes.* That was the first thing he ever said to you. *If I were to draw your face, I'd only want a handful of simple lines. A nose, a mouth, and a pair of eyes, a rough sketch on white paper.* You remember his eyes, large and moist as a calf's. You remember the nervous twist of his lips, his bloodshot eyes as he glanced across at you. *Don't look at me like that,* he would say. *You're scaring me.*

Now

In the lobby of the main building, where the majority of the wards are, all the lights are off. By contrast, light streams out from the entrance to the emergency department, down the side of the annex. In front of this entrance, one of the ambulances from the provincial hospital is parked, with its emergency lights flashing and its rear doors flung open, as though a critical case was rushed here mere seconds before.

The main doors are wide open; you step through and begin to walk down the corridor. You hear low, urgent voices alternating with screams, the rough, mechanical inhalations of medical equipment, the squeal of trolleys being wheeled along linoleum floors. You take a seat on one of the backless chairs in reception.

"What are you here for?" asks the middle-aged woman behind the counter.

"I'm visiting someone."

This isn't true. You haven't arranged any meeting. Visiting hours are only in the mornings, and even then, you have no idea whether Seong-hee would even agree to see you.

A middle-aged man in full hiking gear walks slowly in. He is leaning heavily on the arm of another man, who carries what you assume to be the first man's backpack as well as his own. Judging by the makeshift splint on the former's arm, he seems to have been injured during a nighttime hike. *It's okay*, his friend comforts him, *we're here now*. The expressions contorting their features are surprisingly similar; on second thought, so are those features themselves, so perhaps they aren't friends but brothers. *Not long now. The doctor will be here any minute.*

The doctor will be here any minute.

You remain perched on the edge of your seat, back rigid, listening to the uninjured man repeat those words like a mantra. *The doctor will be here any minute.*

You Remember

You remember the girl who once told you that she wanted to be a doctor, all those years ago.

It was never going to happen; that much had been obvious to you. Jeong-mi was never going to become one of the smart, self-assured medical professionals who marched briskly in and out of hospital wards. She'd told you about her younger brother, Jeong-dae, about how she needed to keep working until she'd seen him through university. By the time he graduated she would already be in her mid-twenties, and even if she started cramming for the middle school exams straightaway . . . but no, the factory would have chewed her up and spat her out long before then. She already suffered from frequent nosebleeds, and a cough she seemed unable to shake. With legs as skinny as young radishes she darted among the sewing machines, snatching a few minutes of sleep here and there by leaning against a pillar and slipping under with all the abruptness of the anesthetized. *How can you survive in such a din?* she'd shouted. *I can't even hear myself think.* Eyes wide with fear, stunned by the sewing machines' almighty clamor, on her very first day in that job.

Now

The tang of bleach spikes your nostrils in the hospital bathroom. You run the taps, and take a swig from your water bottle while the sink fills. After you've finished washing your face, you give your teeth a vigorous brushing. Washing your hair with the hand soap and drying it with a hand towel reminds you of the sit-ins you used to go on with Seong-hee. You've brought a lotion sample with you, in your cotton wash bag. You tear open the packaging and smear the gel onto your pallid cheeks.

When you and Seong-hee spoke on the phone the previous Monday, her voice had sounded so altered that you were momentarily unable to picture her face. Only after you'd hung up did you recall her bright, intelligent eyes, the sliver of pink gum that was revealed whenever she smiled. But of course, ten years have gone by, and that face must be as changed as her voice. Gaunt with illness as well as age. Right now, she will be asleep. Her breathing will be low and labored, punctuated by snores like the snuffling of a sick animal.

You Remember

You remember that night in the dead of winter, in the attic room of a two-story house belonging to an American pastor who ministered to the factory workers—a place where the police couldn't just rush in whenever they felt like it, and where Seong-hee had sought shelter for a number of years in her twenties—where you abandoned any sense of impropriety and slept with your body jammed up against hers. You remember that Seong-hee had snored the whole night through, which had jarred with the usual impression she gave of gentle earnestness. You tried pressing up against the wall, tried pulling the mothball-scented quilt right up over your head, but nothing could block out those deafening snores.

Now

Hunched up in the corner where two rows of chairs meet, hugging your backpack to yourself, you slide into a shallow sleep. Every time some external sound startles you and the fabric of sleep wears thin, the repeated words from Yoon's e-mail, a pianist hammering the same keys, flicker in your mind's eye like a cursor blinking on a computer screen. Testimony. Meaning. Memory. For the future.

The nerves threading your eyeballs spark into life, slender as lightbulb filaments, and your eyelids blink open. With the muscles of your face still heavy with drowsiness, you turn to examine the dimly lit corridor, the deep dark beyond the glass door. Again, you experience that moment when the contours of suffering coalesce into clarity, a clarity colder and harder than any nightmare could ever be. The moment when you are forced to acknowledge that what you experienced was no mere dream.

Yoon has asked you to remember. To "face up to those memories," to "bear witness to them."

But how can such a thing be possible?

Is it possible to bear witness to the fact of a foot-long wooden ruler being repeatedly thrust into my vagina, all the way up to the back wall of my uterus? To a rifle butt bludgeoning my cervix? To the fact that, when the bleeding wouldn't stop and I had gone into shock, they had to take me to the hospital for a blood transfusion? Is it possible to face up to my continuing to bleed for the next two years, to a blood clot forming in my Fallopian tubes and leaving me permanently unable to bear children? It is possible to bear witness to the fact that I ended up with a pathological aversion to physical contact, particularly with men? To the fact that someone's lips merely grazing mine, their hand brushing my cheek, even so

much as a casual gaze running up my legs in summer, was like being seared
with a branding iron? Is it possible to bear witness to the fact that I ended
up despising my own body, the very physical stuff of my self? That I will-
fully destroyed any warmth, any affection whose intensity was more than
I could bear, and ran away? To somewhere colder, somewhere safer. Purely
to stay alive.

Only a portion of the emergency department is visible from
where you are sitting, but this is constantly lit by the harsh glare of
strip lighting. Someone starts moaning, either a child or a young
woman. Impossible to tell. Then the raised voices of a middle-
aged couple, most likely the parents. Hasty footsteps, and you see
a nurse running.

You shoulder your backpack, stand up, and walk outside. Two
ambulances, their emergency lights off, are huddled together beneath a chill light. The wind has lost its clammy warmth. Finally,
the heat has abated.

You walk along the tarmac for a while, then step to the side,
onto the grass where it is apparently forbidden to tread. You take
a diagonal line across the grass, heading for the main building.
Your trainer socks leave your ankles exposed, brushed by the tips
of the moisture-beaded grass. You inhale deeply, the impending
rain bringing out the rich, loamy base notes of the soil. About
halfway across the grass, the faces of the two girls slide into your
mind. Lying side by side, a banner resting on their chests. Their
sleepy faces as they lift the banner up over their heads and put
it aside, rise to their feet, and come stepping lightly over the
grass. Your throat is dry. There is a bitter taste at the back of
your mouth, even though you brushed your teeth only an hour

ago. What lies beneath the dark grass, what you are continuing to tread on, seems not soil but fine, sharp splinters of glass.

Up Rising

After that night, I stopped hanging the wet towel on the door handle.

And yet all through that winter, and even in the spring, when the air was no longer so dry and there would have been no need for a wet towel anyway, I continued to hear that sound, seeming to come from just the other side of the door.

Even now, those occasional times when I manage to awake from a sleep that was free from nightmares, I hear it.

Each time, my eyes tremble open and I face out into the darkness.

Who is it?

Who's there?

Who is coming toward me, and with such soft footsteps?

You Remember

All the buildings have their shutters down.

All the windows are closed and locked.

Suspended above the darkened street, the seventeenth-day moon hangs in the sky like an eyeball formed of ice, peering down on the van you are riding in.

It was mainly the female students who rode around with megaphones to do the street broadcasts. When those with you were completely spent, when they said it felt as though their throats had closed up and could no longer produce anything louder than a whisper, you took over for forty minutes. *Brothers and sisters, please turn on your lights.* That was the kind of thing you said. Addressing the blind windows, the deserted alleyways. *For God's sake, please just turn on your lights.*

The reason the soldiers let you ride around broadcasting all day, waiting until the dead of night before forcing your van to a halt and arresting all its occupants, only occurred to you later: they simply hadn't wanted to expose their movements. The women, the ones who'd been doing the actual broadcasting, were hauled off to the cells at Gwangsan police station, while the man who had been in charge of driving was taken to the military school. You were carrying a gun at the time of your arrest, and so you were kept separate from the other women, and transferred to the custody of the military police.

There, the only name by which you were referred to was "Red Bitch." Because you used to be a factory girl, and had been involved in the labor union movement. Their script decreed that the four years you'd spent at a dressmaker's in what they called "a provincial city" had been a mere cover, that you were a spy sent down from the communist North. It was to elicit the confession that would confirm these accusations that they had you lie down on the table in the interrogation room, day after day. *Filthy Red Bitch. Scream as much as you like, who's going to come running?* Tube lighting flickered along the ceiling of the interrogation room. Beneath the flat, banal brightness of that perfectly innocuous light, they kept at you until the hemorrhaging had gone on for so long, you were finally released from feeling.

Around a year after you got out of there, you saw Seong-hee

again. You went to the Industrial Mission Church to ask after her whereabouts, got in contact, and arranged to meet at a noodle place in Guro-dong. Listening to your story, she seemed surprised.

"It never even occurred to me that you might be in prison. I just presumed you were living quietly somewhere, trying to put the past behind you."

Repeated stretches either in prison or on the run, arrested and later released only to be pursued again for further acts of agitation, had left Seong-hee's cheeks so sunken she was barely recognizable as the same person. She was twenty-seven when you met her then, and could easily have passed for ten years older. She stayed silent for a while, as the steam rose from her cooling noodles.

"Jeong-mi disappeared that spring; did you know?" This time you are the one to look surprised. "I heard she helped out with the union for a while. We were blacklisted, of course, so she quit her job at the factory before they had the chance to lay her off. After that, I didn't hear anything more . . . in fact, I only recently heard about her disappearing. The woman who told me used to attend night classes with her when they both worked at a textiles factory in Gwangju."

You stare, mute, at the shapes formed by Seong-hee's mouth. As though your mother tongue has been rendered opaque, a meaningless jumble of sounds.

The words you are struggling for refuse to come. You can't even remember the girl's face with any clarity. The effort to remember is wearing you out. Fragments surface momentarily, only to disappear from whence they came. Pale skin. A compact set of small white teeth. *I want to be a doctor.*

Nothing else.

Up Rising

I went back to Gwangju to die.

For a little while after I got out of prison my older brother let me stay with him out in the countryside, but the police had his address on file, and their twice-weekly visits were too much for me.

One morning in early February, when the sun hadn't yet come up, I put on the smartest clothes I had, packed a bag with a few basic necessities, and went out to catch one of the intercity buses.

At first glance the city looked as though it hadn't changed a jot. But it didn't take me long to see that, actually, nothing was the same anymore. There were bullet holes in the outer wall of the Provincial Office. The people moving through the streets in their somber clothes all had something twisted about their faces, as though they were contorted with transparent scars. I walked among them, my shoulders jostling theirs. I didn't get hungry, didn't get thirsty, and my feet didn't get cold either. It seemed like I could have gone on walking that whole day through, all through the night until the sun came up.

That was when I saw you, Dong-ho.

I was looking at the photos some students had recently pinned up on the wall of the Catholic Center on the main road leading to the Provincial Office.

The police were a constant menace. Even then, I was aware that one of them might be hiding nearby, watching me. I hurriedly pulled down one of the photos, rolled it up tight, and clenched it in my fist. I crossed the main street and disappeared down an alleyway. There was a sign for a music café, so I hastened up the stairs to the fifth floor, took a seat in the cavernous room, and ordered a coffee. I sat there stock-still until the waiter had set my coffee down in front of me and left me alone. The acoustics were excellent in such a large space, yet I was hardly aware of a single note. It was like being *submerged in deep water. Eventually, once I was sure that I was completely alone, I unclenched my fist and smoothed out the photograph.*

You were lying on your side in the yard of the Provincial Office. The force of the gunshot had splayed your limbs. Your face and chest were exposed to the sky, while your knees were pressed against the ground. I could see how you must have suffered in those final moments, from the way you were twisted like that.

I couldn't breathe.

Couldn't make a sound.

That summer, you were dead. While the blood was still hemorrhaging out of my body, the rot was running furiously through yours, packed into the earth.

What I saw in the photograph saved me. You saved me, Dong-ho, you made my blood seethe back to life. The force of my suffering surged through me in a fury that seemed it would burst my heart.

Now

At the entrance to the car park for the main hospital building, the lights are on in the security hut. You peer in at the elderly guard, sleeping the night through with his head tipped back over the top of his swivel chair, his mouth hanging open. A dust-clouded bulb is suspended from the ceiling of the hut. A scattering of dead flies litters the cement floor. The sun will soon be up. It will pulse gradually brighter, glaring fiercely down on the city it holds in its grip. Everything that has lost the life it once had will rapidly putrefy. A foul stench will waft in waves from every alley where rubbish has been dumped.

You remember that hushed exchange between Dong-ho and Eun-sook, all those years ago. Why do they cover corpses with the Taegukgi, Dong-ho had wanted to know, why sing the national anthem? You can't recall Eun-sook's answer.

And if he were asking you? If he were asking now? *To wrap them in the Taegukgi—we wanted to do that much for them, at least. We needed the national anthem for the same reason we needed the minute's silence. To make the corpses we were singing over into something more than butchered lumps of meat.*

Twenty years lie between that summer and now. *Red bitches, we're going to exterminate the lot of you.* But you've turned your back on all that. On spat curses, the abrupt smack of water against skin. The door leading back to that summer has been slammed shut; you've made sure of that. But that means that the way is also closed that might have led back to the time before. There is no way back to the world before the torture. No way back to the world before the massacre.

Up Rising

I don't know who the footsteps belong to.

Whether it's always the same person, or someone different every time.

Maybe they don't come one at a time. Maybe that's something they've left behind, now, their individual identities merging into a body with only the barest trace of mass, the merest quivered hint at an outer boundary. Countless existences, blurring into vagueness like ink in water.

You Remember

Only occasionally, just now and then, you wonder.

Some weekend afternoon when the sun-drenched scene outside the window seems unusually still and Dong-ho's profile flits into your mind, mightn't the thing flickering in front of your eyes be what they call a soul? In the early hours of the morning, when dreams you can't remember have left your cheeks wet and the contours of that face jolt into an abrupt clarity, mightn't that wavering be a soul's emergence? And the place they emerge from, that they waver back into, would it be black as night or dusk's coarse weave? Dong-ho, Jin-su, the bodies that your own hands washed and dressed, might they be gathered in that place, or are they sundered, several, scattered?

You are aware that, as an individual, you have the capacity for neither bravery nor strength.

After the policeman stamped on your stomach, you chose to leave the labor union. After you got out of jail, you rejoined Seong-hee for a while in the labor movement, but you went against her advice in transferring to the environmental organization, which was quite different in character from Seong-hee's union. Afterward, you chose not to seek her out again even while knowing how much this would wound her. The Dictaphone and tapes in the backpack, which is cutting into your shoulders, will, after all this, wind up in the post to Yoon as soon as you can get to the post office on Monday morning. Unused.

But at the same time you know that if a time like that spring were to come around again, and even knowing what you know now, you might well end up making a similar choice to the one you'd made then. Like those times during a primary school dodge-ball game when, having nimbly avoided danger thus far, there was no one but you left standing on your team and you had to face up to the challenge of catching the ball. Like the time your feet led you to the square, drawn there by the resonant song of the young women on the bus, even though you knew that armed soldiers were stationed there. Like that final night when they asked who was willing to stay until the end and you quietly raised your hand. *We mustn't let ourselves become victims,* Seong-hee had said. *We mustn't let them dismiss us like that.* That spring night with the moon's watchful eye silently bearing witness to the girls gathered on the roof. Who was it who slipped that sliver of peach between your lips? You can't recall.

Now

You walk away from the hospital's main building. The morning's half-light comes creeping over the grass as you cut back across it. You slide both hands beneath the straps of the backpack, its dragging weight like a lump of iron. Like a child you're carrying on your back. So perhaps your hands are supporting, comforting, the backpack a baby's sling.

I'm the one who's responsible, aren't I?

You ask this of the blue-tinged darkness undulating around you.

If I'd demanded that you go home, Dong-ho; if I'd begged, while we sat there eating gimbap, you would have done as I asked, wouldn't you?

And that's why you're coming to me now.

To ask why I'm still alive.

You walk, your eyes' red rims seeming carved with some keen blade. Hurrying back to the bright lights of the emergency department.

There's only one thing for me to say to you, onni.

If you'll allow me to.

If you'll please allow me.

The streetlights lining the road that branches off to the funeral hall and the emergency department, the main building and the annex, all switch themselves off at exactly the same time. As you walk along the straight white line that follows the center of the road, you raise your head to the falling rain.

Don't die.

Just don't die.

6

The Boy's Mother, 2010

I followed you as soon as I spotted you, Dong-ho.

You had a good head of steam on, whereas I'm a bit doddery these days. Would I ever catch you up? If you'd turned your head just a little to the side, I'd have been able to see your profile, but you just kept going, for all the world as though there was something driving you on.

Middle-school boys all had their hair cut short back then, didn't they, but it seems to have gone out of fashion now. That's how I knew it had to be you—I'd know that round little chestnut of a head anywhere. It was you, no mistake. Your brother's hand-me-down school uniform was like a sack on you, wasn't it? It took you till the third year to finally grow into it. In the mornings when you slipped out through the main gate with your book bag, and your clothes so neat and clean, ah, I could have gazed on that sight all day. This kid didn't have any book bag with him; the hands swinging by his sides were empty. Well, he must have put it down somewhere. There was no mistaking those toothpick arms, poking out of your short shirtsleeves. It was your narrow shoulders, your own special way of walking, loping like a little fawn with your head thrust slightly forward. It was definitely you.

You'd come back to me this one time, come back to let your mother catch just a glimpse of you, and this doddery old woman couldn't even catch you up. An hour I spent searching among the market stalls, down the alleyways, and you weren't there. My knees were throbbing something awful and I felt dizzy as a whirligig, so I just plumped right down on the ground where I was. But I knew if someone from the neighborhood saw me there, they'd be bound to kick up a fuss, so I pushed myself to my feet even though my head was still swimming.

Following you all the way into the market alleys, I guess I hadn't realized what a distance I'd come; getting back home was such a slog that my throat was soon parched. Of course, I'd gone and come out without so much as a single coin in my pocket, so all I could think of was to stick my head into the nearest shop and cadge a glass of water. Then again, they might think I was some old beggar-woman come to bother them. So I just had to keep on walking, supporting myself against the wall whenever there was one to hand. I shuffled by the construction site with my hand clamped tightly over my mouth. There was dust flying all over the place, and it set me coughing. How had I not noticed it when I'd gone by in the other direction? Somewhere where there was such an almighty racket as all that, where the road was being carved up.

Last summer the torrential rain made potholes in the alley in front of our house. The kids from the neighborhood were forever losing their footing there, and if the wheel of a stroller accidentally went in, it was in danger of never coming out again. In the end, the city council sent some people to re-lay the tarmac. This was early September, when some days were still real scorchers. They fetched the boiling tarmac in a wheelbarrow, bubbling like a stew. Poured it down, smoothed it out, and gave it a good trampling until it'd firmed up.

On the evening the workmen finally packed up their stuff and left, I thought I'd just go and have a look at it. They'd strung a thin rope barrier around the newly laid tarmac, though, so I kept to the edges and tried to tread as lightly as possible. I could feel my battered old body slowly absorbing its warmth like a tree sucks up water: first my ankles, then my calves, then my aching knee joints. The next morning the rope was gone, so I ventured out onto the surface. It was much warmer in the center than the edges had been, flooding into me like a wave. I walked right the way up and down the alley after lunch and dinner, and the next morning, too. Your elder brother and his wife were down from Seoul, and I could see her wondering what'd got into me. "Wouldn't you like to sit down, Mother?" she asked. "That tarmac must still be awfully hot . . ."

"Ah, the cold's deep in my bones. Do you know how warm this stuff is? It'll do my joints a world of good."

Your brother shook his head, murmuring to himself about how something wasn't right with me. He'd been suggesting I move in with him for a few years now. "Where did she run off to?" I heard him mutter.

The tarmac held its heat for three days straight, but eventually it cooled down. Nothing to feel regretful over there, I knew, but I couldn't help wishing it'd stayed. All the same, I'd wander out there after lunch to stand on it for a bit and wait. *After all, I thought, it might still be just that bit warmer than other places.* And if I stood there and kept a good look out, who's to say I wouldn't spot you again, striding by like the last time?

I can't get my head around why I didn't just call your name that day. Why I just came tottering on behind, struggling for breath and dumb as a mute. If I call your name next time, will you please just turn around? You don't need to say "Yes, Mum?" or anything like that. Just turn round so I can see you.

But it wasn't really you, was it?

No.

It can't have been.

I buried you with my own two hands. Removed your PE jacket and your sky-blue tracksuit bottoms, and dressed you in your dark winter uniform, over a white shirt. Tightened your belt just so and put clean gray socks on you. When they put you in a plywood coffin and loaded it up onto the rubbish truck, I said I'd ride at the front to watch over you. I didn't have a clue where the truck was heading. I was too busy staring back to the rear, to where you were.

Those hundreds of people in their dark clothes looked like ants carrying coffins up the sandy mound. My memory's hazy, but I can recall your brothers standing there, tears trickling down over lips pressed tight together. The words your father said to me before his death, how stunned he'd been when, instead of crying like all the others, I'd pulled a handful of grass out of the turf they'd removed for the grave, and swallowed it. Swallowed it, sank down to the ground and vomited it back up again then, once it had clawed its way out of me, yanked up another fistful and stuffed it into my mouth. Mind you, I can't remember any of that myself. The stuff that happened before, before the truck carried us off to the cemetery, that's clear enough. More than clear enough. How your face looked that last time, right before the lid was put on the coffin. How ashen it was, how haggard. I'd never realized you were so deathly pale.

Later, your middle brother explained that your face was so white because of all the blood you'd lost when they shot you. And that was why the coffin barely weighed a thing. Not just because you were such a little slip of a thing. Your brother's own eyes were all bloodshot as he ground out the words. *I will pay them back for this evil,* he said, and I can tell you that knocked me for six. *What are you talking about?* I demanded. *How could it ever be possible to "pay back" the evil of the country murdering your brother? If anything were to happen to you, I wouldn't be long for this world.*

And even now thirty years have gone by, on the anniversaries of your and your father's death, I find myself troubled when I watch your brother straighten up after bowing over the offerings. The thin line of his lips, the stoop of his shoulders, the flecks of white in his hair. It's the soldiers, not him, that your death should have weighed on, so why did he grow so old before his time, so much quicker than all his friends? Is he still troubled by thoughts of revenge? Whenever I think this, my heart sinks.

Your eldest brother's quite the opposite, always sure to keep a smile on his face, and never a hint of anything else. Twice a month he comes down to visit, to slip me a little something for the house-keeping and make sure I'm all set up for meals. Then he's back up to Seoul the very same day, so his wife will never even know he was gone. Your middle brother lives practically round the corner, but the eldest has always been kindly by nature.

You, your father, and your eldest brother are all cut from the same cloth, you know. Your long waist and sloping shoulders are a family trait. As for your ever-so-slightly-elongated eyes, your square front teeth, you were a carbon copy of your brother. Even now, when he laughs and reveals those two front teeth, broad and flat as a rabbit's, the look of youthful innocence they give him clashes with the lines etched deeply around his eyes.

Your eldest brother was eleven when you were born. He turned into a teenage girl around you, running home as soon as school was out so he could dandle you on his knee. He cooed over your pretty smile, supported your neck with tender care while he held you in his arms, and rocked you back and forth until you gurgled with delight. After you'd passed your first birthday and he could carry you on his back in a sling, he'd strap you on and proceed to stride around the yard, singing painfully out of tune.

Who would've thought that such a sweet, sensitive boy as that would end up scrapping with your middle brother? That now, more than twenty years down the line, they'd find it so painful even to be in the same room, barely able to exchange more than a handful of words?

It happened three days after your father died, when the eldest had come back home to join us for the grave visit. I was busy in the kitchen when I heard something smash, and when I ran into the main room, there they were going at it, full-grown lads of twenty-seven and thirty-two, panting fit to burst and trying to grab each other by the throat.

"All you had to do was take Dong-ho by the hand and drag him home. What the hell were you thinking of, letting him stay there all that time? How come you let Mother go there on her own that last day? It's all very well to say you could tell that your words were just going in one ear and out the other, but you must have known he would end up dead if he stayed there; you were perfectly aware, how could you let it happen?"

An incoherent, drawn-out howl burst from your middle brother; he flew at the eldest and grappled him to the floor. The pair of them were yowling like animals.

I suppose I could've tried to pull them apart, sat them down, and straightened the whole thing out. Instead, I turned and went back into the kitchen. I didn't want to think about anything. I just carried on flipping pancakes, stirring soup, and threading meat onto skewers.

I can't be sure of anything now.

When I went to see you that last time, what might have happened if you hadn't promised to be back that very evening? If you hadn't spoken to me so gently, setting my mind at ease?

"Dong-ho's promised to be back home after six, when they lock up the gym." That's what I told your father. "He's said we can all have dinner together."

But when seven o'clock came around and there was still no sight of you, your middle brother and I went out to fetch you. Under martial law the curfew started at seven, and the army was due back that evening, so there wasn't so much as a shadow stirring in the streets. It took us a full forty minutes to make it to the gymnasium, but the lights were off and there was no one to be seen. Across the road, some of the civil militia were standing guard in front of the Provincial Office, carrying guns. *I've come to fetch my youngest boy,* I explained, *please, he's expecting me.* Their faces pale and drawn, they insisted that they couldn't allow us in, that no one was permitted to enter. Only the young can be so stubborn, so decisive in the face of their own fear. *The tanks are rolling back into the city as we speak,* they said. *It's dangerous, you need to hurry home.*

"For God's sake," I begged, "let me inside. Or just tell my son we're here. Tell him to come out, just for a moment."

Your brother couldn't stand by any longer; he declared that he'd go and fetch you out himself, but one of the militiamen shook his head.

"If you go in now, that's it, we can't let you back out again. Everyone who's stayed behind has decided to do so at their own risk. They're all prepared to die if they have to."

When your brother raised his voice to say that he understood and was prepared to go in anyway, I quickly cut him off.

"There's no need," I said, "Dong-ho'll come home as soon as he gets the chance. He made me a promise. . . ."

I said it because it was so dark all around us, because I was imagining soldiers springing out of the darkness at any moment. Because I was afraid of losing yet another son.

And that was how I lost you.

I pulled your brother away from the Provincial Office, and the two of us walked back home through those deathly silent streets, with the tears streaming down our faces. Neither of us spoke.

I'll never understand it. The militia with their faces pale and resolute, did they really have to die? When they were just children, really, just children with guns. And why did they refuse to let me in? When they were going to die such futile deaths, what difference could it possibly have made?

• • •

After your brothers have come and gone my days seem that much emptier, and I mostly just sit out on the veranda warming myself in the sun. The quarry just beyond the yard's southern wall might have caused one hell of a din, but at least it meant the place felt nice and open.

We used to live on the other side of the quarry, before we bought this house. The old place was a tiny little slate-roofed affair and could be a bit stuffy, so you and your brothers couldn't wait for Sundays, when the workers had a day off and the three of you could run riot. The big chunks of granite made it prime territory for hide-and-seek, for shouting "the hibiscus has bloomed" at the top of their voices. I could hear them all the way from where I stood in the kitchen. Such rowdy lads, not that you'd have known it once they had another year or so under their belts; they were quiet as anything then.

When your eldest brother moved to Seoul, we decided it was high time for a change of scene. Jeong-mi and Jeong-dae were both so quiet and unassuming, and it was nice to think that here were some friends for you, with you being so much younger than your brothers. There was something comforting about the sight of you and Jeong-dae heading off to school in your identical uniforms, side by side like two peas in a pod. At the weekends when the two of you played badminton in the yard and the shuttlecock inevitably flew over the wall and onto the building site, your game of rock-paper-scissors to decide which of you would go and fetch it never failed to make me smile.

I wonder what became of Jeong-dae and his sister?

When their father came to Gwangju to search for them and started roaming the streets like a madman, I was in no position to offer comfort to anyone. He quit his job and spent a year sleeping in our annex, hanging around the government offices by day. Whenever he heard that a secret grave had been discovered, or that corpses had risen to the surface of some reservoir, he would spring into action. Didn't matter if it was the crack of dawn or the middle of the night.

"They're alive somewhere, I know it. Both of them. They'll turn up one of these days."

I can still picture him staggering into the kitchen after one of his benders, muttering to himself like someone who'd lost his mind. His small face and flat nose. Eyes that used to sparkle with mischief just like his son's, once, before it all went wrong.

He can't have lasted very long after that. When the bodies were exhumed and moved to new graves, the families of the missing set up small cenotaphs; your middle brother went expressly to look for the two kids' names, but apparently they weren't there. If their father had still been alive, surely he would have set up a pair of cenotaphs for them?

Sometimes I wonder whatever possessed us to let the annex out . . . was it all for such a paltry bit of rent? I think about how if Jeong-dae had never set foot in this house, you wouldn't have put your own life at risk trying to find him . . . but then I recall the sound of your laughter on those Sundays when the two of you used to play badminton, and it's my fault, I'm the only one to blame. I shake my head to try and shake all the bad thoughts out. I'm the one with the mark on my conscience, bearing a grudge against those poor kids. I'm the only one to blame.

How pretty she was . . . how pretty, I thought, to have vanished without a trace. That lovely young girl stepping into our house with her arms wrapped around the laundry basket, padding across our yard in her sneakers, with her toothbrush dripping water. Such things seem like the dreams of a previous life.

The thread of life is as tough as an ox tendon, so even after I lost you, it had to go on. I had to make myself eat, make myself work, forcing down each day like a mouthful of cold rice, even if it stuck in my throat.

I'd known about the meetings for bereaved families for some time, of course, but I'd never shown my face there. When I eventually did go, it was because I'd received a phone call from a woman calling herself their representative. Our military thug of a president is coming here to Gwangju, she told me, that butcher dares to set foot in our city . . . when your spilled blood had barely had time to dry.

My sleep was shallow and fitful at the best of times, then, but that news plunged me into a fresh bout of insomnia. Your father was equally disturbed, and what with his delicate constitution and gentle nature I thought it best to have him stay at home while I went to the meeting alone. So I went along to the home of the organizer, who ran a rice shop, introduced myself to the other women, and stayed there until late at night making banners and pickets. Finally, the host decided that we should each go back home, as whatever we didn't have enough of yet could be made just as well there. We shook hands when we said good-bye. We were like scarecrows, shells stuffed with nothing but straw. Our farewells were as hollow as our eyes.

I wasn't frightened.

Death would have been welcome at that point, so what could there possibly have been to fear? When we met up again the next day, to wait for the butcher's convoy, we were each wearing white mourning clothes. The day had hardly got started when the bastard really did show up. Our opportunity had come, to hurl slogans like stones with one voice, and all hell broke loose. We went into a frenzy of howling and fainting, tugging at our hair and tearing at our clothes. No sooner had we rolled out our banners than they were snatched away and the whole lot of us were hauled off to the police station. We were just sitting there in a daze until some young people were brought in; they'd formed their own association, of the wounded, and had been demonstrating at a different spot along the convoy's route. Their faces were sullen when they filed in, until they saw us there.

"Even the mothers are here, too?" one youth wailed, tears streaming down his face. "What crime have they committed?"

In that instant, everything inside my head got blanked out. It was blindingly white, as though the whole world had been painted white. I hitched up my torn skirt and clambered up onto the table.

My voice sounded so much smaller than usual. "That's right," I stammered, "what crime have I committed?"

I jumped down, dashed over to the desk opposite, and scrambled up before anyone had time to blink, the hem of my white skirt fluttering at my ankles. There was a photo of the murderer hanging on the wall—I pulled it down and smashed the glass with my foot. Something splattered across my face—tears, or maybe blood.

The blood kept spurting from my foot, so the policemen had to take me off to the hospital. Your father came to the emergency department after they'd let him know I was there. While the nurse removed the shards of glass from my foot and bandaged the wound, I asked him to do me a favor. "Please go home and look in the wardrobe. There's a banner I made last night but didn't bring with me today."

Around sunset that same day I hobbled up the stairs that led out to the hospital roof, leaning on your father's shoulder for support. I steadied myself against the railing, unfurled the banner, and screamed. *Chun Doo-hwan, you murdered my son. Let's tear that bloodthirsty butcher to pieces.* I carried on screaming until the police came charging up the emergency stairs, seized hold of me, carried me back down to one of the wards, and bundled me into a bed.

We met up frequently after that, determined to carry on the fight. Each time we mothers parted, we clasped hands and brushed shoulders, peering into each other's eyes as we made arrangements to meet again. We even took up a collection so that those who were having trouble making ends meet could afford to hire a bus to go to a meeting in Seoul. One time, some good-for-nothing bastards chucked a smoke grenade inside our bus and one of us collapsed, choking. When the riot police arrested us and forced us into one of those vans with chicken wire over the windows, they pulled over at a secluded spot by the highway and made one of us get out, then drove on for a while before evicting someone else . . . those bastards made sure we were well scattered. I trailed along the side of the road for what felt like an age, completely disoriented. I hadn't the faintest clue where I was. Until finally I stumbled across one of the other women, her lips tinged blue like mine, and we chafed each other's numbed hands.

We made a firm pact to carry on the fight until the end, but the following year your father got ill and I couldn't keep my promise. Watching him facing death that winter, I was bitter. *It's all right for you, you'll soon be out of it. I'm the one who's being left behind, alone in this hell.*

But I don't have a map for whatever world lies beyond death. I don't know whether there, too, there are meetings and partings, whether we still have faces and voices, hearts with the capacity for joy as well as sorrow. How could I tell whether your father's loosening grip on life was something I ought to pity, or to envy?

Winter passes, and spring comes round again. Spring sends me into my usual delirium; summer brings exhaustion and an illness I find difficult to shake off. By the time autumn sets in it's as much as I can do just to keep breathing. And then in winter, of course, my joints stiffen up. The ice that penetrated deep into my bones, into my heart, never leaves me. However sweltering the summer, I never shed a single drop of sweat.

My Dong-ho, I was thirty when I had you. My last-born. My left nipple had been a strange shape for as long as I could remember, and both of your brothers had favored its properly formed partner. My left breast would still swell with milk, of course, but because they refused to suckle from it, it hardened in a way that was completely different from the soft right breast. It was unsightly, a cross I had to bear for several years. But with you, everything was different. You latched on to the left breast of your own free will, your tiny mouth pulling at that deformed nipple with an astonishing gentleness. And so both breasts developed identical soft contours.

My Dong-ho, I never knew a baby could look so happy to be breastfeeding. Or the yellow feces filling the cloth nappy to have such a strangely sweetish scent. You crawled all over the place like a puppy, and there wasn't a thing on earth that you wouldn't put in your mouth. Then there was the time you ran a fever and your face puffed up; you had convulsions and vomited a mess of sour milk onto my chest. After you were weaned, you sucked your thumb with such intensity that the nail wore thin and transparent as paper. You wobbled toward me one step at a time as I clapped and chanted, *Here you come, here you come.* Seven chuckling steps until I could fold you into my arms.

"I don't like summer but I like summer nights": that was something you came out with the year you turned eight. I liked the sound of those words, and I remember thinking to myself, *he'll be a poet.* Times when you three boys sat out on the bench in the yard, sharing watermelon with your father on hot summer nights. When your tongue groped for the sticky-sweet remnants smeared around your mouth.

I cut out the photo from your school ID and put it in my purse. Day or night, the house is always empty, but still I like to wait until the early hours of the morning, when there'd be no earthly reason for anyone to drop by, before I unwrap it from the folds of plain writing paper and smooth out the creases lining your face. There's no one around to overhear, but still I only let myself whisper it . . . *Dong-ho.*

On late autumn days after the rainy season has passed and the sky is startlingly clear, I put my purse in the inside pocket of my jacket and make my slow way down to the riverside, my hands on my knees. I inch along the path where the cosmos blooms in a riot of color, and gadflies swarm on the coils of dead worms.

When you were six or seven, when your brothers were both off at school and the house was quiet even at one o'clock in the afternoon, you were so bored you didn't know what to do with yourself. So each day the two of us walked along the riverside, all the way to the shop to see your father. You disliked the shadowed places where the trees blocked out the sun. When I wanted to walk there to escape the heat, you tugged me by the wrist as hard as you could, back to where it was bright. Even though your fine hair sparkled with sweat, and you were panting so hard you sounded as if you were in pain. *Let's walk over there, Mum, where it's sunny, we might as well, right?* Pretending that you were too strong for me, I let you pull me along. *It's sunny over there, Mum, and there's lots of flowers, too. Why are we walking in the dark, let's go over there, where the flowers are blooming.*

The Writer, 2013

I was nine years old at the time of the Gwangju Uprising.

That year, we'd just moved up from Gwangju to Suyuri, on the outskirts of Seoul. There, I would hole myself up and pore over whichever book I could lay my hands on, spend entire afternoons playing *omok* with my brothers, or sigh my way through various small tasks such as peeling garlic or deheading anchovies—the kinds of chores I hated most, but which were the ones my mother reserved for me. It was during this time that I overheard snatches of the grown-ups' conversation.

"Was he one of your kids?" my father's sister asked him, one Sunday in early autumn while they were having dinner.

"I wasn't his form teacher, but I took him for some other classes. He always did a good job of the creative writing, I remember that. When we sold the *hanok* and moved, I introduced myself to the new buyer as a teacher at D middle school; the man was really glad to meet me, told me his youngest was in the first year there, but he had to mention the name several times before it clicked. I only really knew him to look at, from when I'd taken the register for their class."

Beyond that, I don't remember exactly what was said. I remember only the expressions on their faces; the struggle to get through the story while having to skirt around the most gruesome parts; the awkward, drawn-out silences. However many times the subject was changed to something a little lighter, the conversation always seemed to circle back around to that initial, unspoken center, seemingly in spite of the speakers. I became oddly tense, straining to catch the words. I already knew that one of the students my father had taught had lived in the *hanok* after us; that was no great secret. So why were they lowering their voices? Why, just before that boy's name was uttered, did an unaccountable silence wedge itself in?

It was a typical old-style *hanok*, with the rooms arranged around a central courtyard, sliding paper doors, and a tiled roof. In the center of the courtyard was a flower bed with a stumpy camellia plant. Every year when the hot weather set in, rose creepers swept their carpet of blossoms up the wall, the petals so dark red they were almost black. Later, when the roses withered, the white hollyhocks surged up the wall of the annex to the height of a grown adult. The iron bars of the main gate were painted a pale straw color; when you pushed it open to go out, you could see the top of the battery factory. I remember the morning we moved: my father and uncle padding the corners of the paulownia wardrobe with a quilt, their movements deft and skillful.

Seoul, January 1980—I wouldn't have believed anywhere could be so cold. Before moving out to Suyuri we spent three months in a tenement building, where the walls might as well have been made of plywood for all the good they did retaining heat.

It was barely any warmer inside than out, and our breath puffed out of us in white clouds. Even huddled in a coat and with a quilt pulled around you, your teeth chattered audibly.

All through that winter, my thoughts kept straying back to our old *hanok*. Not that there was anything bad about the new house. I simply didn't feel that attached to it, probably as we'd only lived there for a relatively short time. The *hanok*, on the other hand, was where I'd spent the first nine years of my life. My grandfather had bought it for my mother, his only daughter. If you wanted to step across from the veranda into the kitchen, you had to pass through my tiny room. In summer I lay there to do my homework with my stomach pressed against the floor. On winter afternoons, I would slide the paper door open a fraction and peer out into the courtyard, where a clean wash of sunlight was puddled on the paving stones.

It was early summer when they came to the house in Suyuri.

At some point between 3 and 4 a.m., Mum shook me awake. *Get up, I'm switching the light on.* The light flicked on before I even had time to blink. I sat up, rubbing my eyes. Two men were standing in the room, their broad shoulders outlined against the black rectangle of the open door. "These men have come from the estate agent's," Mum told me. She was still in her pajamas. "To look at the house."

I was instantly wide awake. Clinging to Mum, I watched wide-eyed as the men rummaged through the wardrobe, searched under the desk, and climbed up into the loft, carrying flashlights. It didn't make sense. Why would men from the estate agent's need to look inside the wardrobe? And why would they come by in the middle of the night? After a while, one of the men came down from the loft and led Mum into the kitchen. When I hesitantly followed them, she turned and mouthed, *you lot stay here*. Her eyes gave nothing away. When I looked back over my shoulder, I saw that my two brothers had wandered into the room in their pajamas. The look on their faces was blank and uncomprehending. My father's voice was low but resonant, coming from the main room. There was no door between the kitchen and my room, just a lace curtain, but whatever my mother was saying to the man, it was so quiet I couldn't make out a single word.

When our extended family gathered for the thanksgiving festival that autumn, the grown-ups took care to keep their voices down whenever they were talking among themselves. So that my brothers and I, and even our younger cousins, wouldn't overhear anything we weren't supposed to. As though we children were spies.

My father's brother was working in the defense industry at the time, and the two of them whispered together in the main room until the small hours.

"Please, *hyeong*, be careful. I'm pretty sure they've tapped your phone line. These days, whenever I call you I can hear this kind of whooshing sound; that's wiretapping. My friend Yeong-jun— you remember him, right? He's decided to get out of it while he still can. The military police took him the year before last, and pried off every single one of his fingernails. Another round of that would finish him off."

Hushed voices from the kitchen; the younger wives preparing food with my mother.

"The guy who bought your *hanok* was renting the annex out

to a couple of kids; the boy was in the same year as the landlord's son. I heard that there's three dead and two missing from D middle school alone . . . including both the kids who were living there."

My mother merely bowed her head in silence. It took a while before she began to speak, and when she did her voice was so low I could barely make it out.

"There was a young woman . . . she was waiting for her husband outside their house. Not long before her due date. They shot her in the middle of the head. She died instantly."

In my impressionable child's imagination, I saw a woman in her twenties standing in front of our old *hanok*'s main gate, her hands on her round stomach. A bullet hole opened up in the center of her pale forehead. Wide as a surprised eye.

Two summers on, my father brought the photo chapbook home.

He'd been down to Gwangju on a condolence call, and had picked it up at the train station—they were relatively common at the time, though printed in secret and sold unofficially. Once the grown-ups had finished passing around the book, the silence that ensued was heavy as lead. Father put it away in the bookcase, up on the highest shelf so we children wouldn't accidentally come across it. He even slid it in back-to-front, so that the spine wasn't visible.

At night, though, when the grown-ups were all sitting in the kitchen and I knew I'd be safe at least until the end of the nine o'clock news, I crept into the main room in search of that book. I scanned every spine until finally I got to the top shelf; I still re-member the moment when my gaze fell upon the mutilated face of a young woman, her features slashed through with a bayonet.

Soundlessly, and without fuss, some tender thing deep inside me broke. Something that, until then, I hadn't even realized was there.

The floor of the gymnasium had been dug up.

I stood looking down at the exposed earth. Large windows were set into each of the four walls. The Taegukgi was still hanging in its frame on the wall. I walked over to the opposite wall, the semifrozen earth packed solid beneath my feet. On the laminated A4 notice, a single phrase had been printed in cursive script. *Please remove your shoes before exercising.*

When I turned to look back at the main door, I noticed the stairs leading up to the first floor. As I walked up, my shoes left deep impressions in the thick layer of dust. The gallery was lined with rows of concrete seating, with a view of the entire gymnasium. When I sat down and breathed out, a cloud of condensation dissolved in the air. The concrete's chill leached through the fabric of my jeans. Corpses wrapped in makeshift shrouds, plywood coffins covered with the Taegukgi, wailing children and blank-faced women, wavered briefly into view over the dark red earth.

I started too late, I thought. I should have come before they dug up the floor. Before the whole frontage of the Provincial Office was masked with scaffolding, with signs reading "Under Construction." Before the majority of the gingko trees, which had borne mute witness to it all, were uprooted. Before the hundred-and-fifty-year-old pagoda tree withered and died.

But I'm here now.

I'll zip up my hooded top and stay here until the sun goes down. Until the outlines of the boy's face solidify. Until I hear his voice in my mind. Until his retreating figure begins to hover over the invisible floorboards, flickering like a candle's guttering flame.

My younger brother still lives in Gwangju. Two days ago, I arrived at his apartment and unpacked my stuff. I arranged for the two of us to have dinner together when he got home from work, then went to see the old *hanok* while it was still light. I hadn't lived in Gwangju since I was a child, so I wasn't really sure where anything was. I got the taxi to take me to H primary school first, which I'd attended up to the third year. Turning my back on the main entrance, I walked over the pedestrian crossing then headed left, groping through memories for some sense of familiarity. The stationery shop I remembered was still there—or, if not the same shop exactly, then at least the same line of business. I walked a little farther on, then, yes, that was it; I had to take a right. I chose the second right after the stationer's, trusting to the spatial memory embedded in my muscles. The wall of the battery factory, which once seemed to stretch on forever, was gone now. Even the row of *hanok* buildings that used to face it had disappeared. Where that street joined the main road there'd been a quarry the length and breadth of a house, sharing a wall with our old *hanok*. There was no way a quarry, essentially just a tract of vacant land, would have been left undeveloped so near the center of this city of now over a million inhabitants.

Past single-story houses and larger tenement buildings, a piano academy and a shop selling engraved seals, I finally arrived at the end of the street. The three-story concrete building standing on the site of the former quarry was something of an eyesore. Our old *hanok* had been pulled down, and in its place was a two-story prefab—a shop selling fixtures and fittings.

What had I been expecting? I hung around in front of that shop for a long time, as though I'd arranged to meet someone there.

Yesterday, the day after that visit to the site of the old house, I made an early start. I went first to the 5:18 Research Institute at Jeonnam University, and the related Cultural Foundation. The main entrance to the military police headquarters, where the central intelligence agency had been stationed since the 1970s and where torture had been carried out, was locked, making it impossible to go inside.

In the afternoon I went to D middle school. At first I'd thought of looking through the yearbooks for the boy's photo, but then I remembered that, of course, he'd never made it to graduation. I called up the retired art teacher, who'd spent his entire working life at that school and was an old friend of my father's, and he arranged permission for me to look through the school's records, where they kept a photograph of every former student. There I saw his face for the first time. There was something meek and gentle about those single-lidded half-moon eyes. The traces of infancy still lingered in the soft line of his jaw. It was a face so utterly ordinary you could easily have mistaken it for that of another, a face whose characteristics would be forgotten the moment you turned away from it.

When I left the staffroom and crossed the exercise yard, streaks of white were just beginning to appear in the leaden sky.

By the time I reached the school gates the snow was coming down in earnest. I brushed away the flakes clinging to my eyelashes, hailed a taxi, and, when one pulled over, asked him to take me back to Jeonnam University. I seemed to recall having seen a similar face in the exhibition hall at the 5:18 Institute.

The exhibition featured several small wall-mounted screens, each one showing a different video on a loop. Since I couldn't remember in what context I'd seen the face, I had to go around and watch each video from the beginning. It was when they were showing one of the earliest marches, when the bodies of the youths who had been gunned down at the station were being pushed in a handcart, that I spotted the figure of what was surely another middle-schooler. The boy was standing at some distance from the head of the column, staring at the corpses with the stunned look of someone who had just been struck in the face. This had all happened in late spring, yet he was hugging himself as if for warmth. The scene skipped on in a matter of seconds, so I stood and waited for the film to return to the beginning. I watched the whole thing two, three, four times. The boy's face was every bit as generic, as mistakable as the one from the school records. I just couldn't be sure. Perhaps, back then, boys with short hair in school uniform all looked much the same? Perhaps they all had such gentle single-lidded eyes. Such skinny gangling limbs, poised for the growth spurt into manhood.

My initial intention was to read each and every document I could get my hands on. From early December onward I abandoned all other work, even avoided seeing friends if I possibly could, just obsessively ploughed through reams of documents. After two months of this, by the time January was drawing to a close, I felt unable to continue.

It was because of the dreams.

In one dream I was being chased by a gang of soldiers. My breathing grew ragged as they gained on me. One of them shoved me in the back and knocked me onto my front. As soon as I rolled over and looked up at my attacker, he thrust his bayonet into my chest, smack bang into my solar plexus. At two o'clock in the morning I jerked awake, sat bolt upright, and placed my hand on my breastbone. I spent the next five minutes struggling to breathe. When I passed my hand over my face my palm came away glistening; I hadn't even been aware that I was crying.

A few days later someone came to see me. "In the thirty-three years between 1980 and now," this person said, "dozens of 5:18 arrestees have been held in secret underground rooms. Tomorrow, at three o'clock in the afternoon, and without any of this having been made public, they are all due to be executed." In the dream it was eight o'clock in the evening—only nineteen hours remaining until the planned execution. How could I stop it from happening? The person who had told me all this had disappeared somewhere, and I was standing in the middle of the street clutching my cell phone, totally at a loss. Should I call someone official, some kind of authority, and let them know what was about to take place? Even once I'd informed them, would they be able to stop it from going ahead? Why had this knowledge come to me of all people, someone who had no power whatsoever? *Where should I go, how can I . . .* as these words were smoldering inside my mouth, my eyes snapped open. Another dream. Just a dream. As I eased my clenched fists open I was muttering to myself in the darkness, *only a dream, only a dream.*

Another dream: Someone makes me a present of a handheld radio. This is a time machine, they tell me, explaining that you are supposed to enter a given year, month, and day in the digital panel. I key in "5:18.1980." After all, if I wanted to describe it in a book, then what better way than to actually experience it for myself? But the next moment I find myself standing alone at the intersection by Gwanghwamun Station. The vast streets are deserted. *Of course, because it's only the time that changes. And I'm in Seoul, not Gwangju.* I'd set the date to May so it ought to be spring, yet the streets were as cold and desolate as certain days in November. Frighteningly still.

A wedding I was obliged to attend took me out of the house for the first time in a long while. January 2013, and the streets of Seoul were just as they had been in my dream of a few days before. The wedding hall was festooned with glittering chandeliers. There was something shockingly incongruous about the people there, their flamboyant clothes, the way they were laughing as though nothing was wrong. How was such a scene possible, when so many people had died? I bumped into a critic, who jokingly took me to task for not having sent him my story collection. I couldn't make sense of it. Not with so many dead. Unable to come up with a good enough excuse not to join the others for lunch after the ceremony, I simply chose my moment and slipped away.

· · ·

The sky was so clear, the recent snow seemed scarcely believable. Oblique shafts of afternoon sunlight slant in through the windows of the gymnasium.

I stand up, chilled by the concrete seating, descend the stairs, open the door, and step outside. I stare at the huge scaffolding filling my field of vision, at the corner of white wall that it leaves exposed. I'm waiting. No one is going to come, but still I wait. No one even knows I'm here, but I'm waiting all the same.

I remember the winter when I was twenty, when I went alone to the hilltop cemetery in Mangwol-dong for the first time. I walked among the graves, looking for him. At the time, I didn't know his family name. The only information I had was that he was called Dong-ho, a name that had easily lodged itself in my memory as it was similar to that of my uncle. And also that he had died at fifteen.

I missed the last bus going back to the city center, so I had to walk along the darkening road with the wind at my back. After I'd been walking for some time I realized that I'd unconsciously placed my right hand on the left-hand side of my chest. As though my heart had fissured open. As though this were something I could carry around with me in perfect safety, as long as I held it tight.

There were soldiers who were especially cruel.

When I first started poring over the documents, what had proved most incomprehensible was that this bloodshed had been committed again and again, and with no attempt to bring the perpetrators before the authorities. Acts of violence committed in broad daylight, without hesitation and without regret. Commanding officers who would have encouraged, no, even demanded such displays of brutality.

In autumn 1979, when the democratic uprising in the southern cities of Busan and Masan was being suppressed, President Park Chung-hee's chief bodyguard Cha Ji-cheol said to him, *The Cambodian government's killed another 2 million of theirs. There's nothing stopping us from doing the same.* In May 1980, when the demonstrations were gathering force in Gwangju, the army used flamethrowers against unarmed citizens. The soldiers were provided with lead bullets, despite these having been banned by the international court of law on humanitarian grounds. Chun Doo-hwan, who had been so much in Park Chung-hee's confidence that he was known as the former president's adopted son, was looking into sending in Special Forces and subjecting the city to aerial bombardment in the unlikely event of the Provincial Office holding out. On the morning of May 21, not long before the army opened fire on the massed crowds, he was seen arriving in a military helicopter and stepping out onto the ground of Gwangju. I saw him on the news: the young general with his air of self-possession. Striding briskly forward from the helicopter, greeting the officer who came forward to meet him with a firm handshake.

I read an interview with someone who had been tortured; they described the aftereffects as "similar to those experienced by victims of radioactive poisoning." Radioactive matter lingers for decades in muscle and bone, causing chromosomes to mutate. Cells turn cancerous, life attacks itself. Even if the victim dies, even if their body is cremated, leaving nothing but the charred remains of bone, that substance cannot be obliterated.

In January 2009, when an illegal raid by riot police on activists and tenants protesting their forced eviction from central Seoul left six dead, I remember being glued to the television, watching the towers burning in the middle of the night and surprising myself with the words that sprang from my mouth: *But that's Gwangju*. In other words, "Gwangju" had become another name for whatever is forcibly isolated, beaten down, and brutalized, for all that has been mutilated beyond repair. The radioactive spread is ongoing. Gwangju had been reborn only to be butchered again in an endless cycle. It was razed to the ground, and raised up anew in a bloodied rebirth.

And there is still that young woman's face.

That young woman whose photograph had made such a terrible impression on my eleven-year-old eyes, dead with a bayonet wound from her cheek to her throat, one eye cracked open and the other closed.

When those wretched corpses were lying in the waiting room of the bus terminal, sprawled in front of the train station; when the soldiers fell upon passersby, beat them, stripped them to their underwear and forced them into a truck; when even the youths who'd stayed quietly at home were ferreted out and arrested; when the roads into the city were blockaded, and the phone lines were cut; when live shells were fired at crowds protesting with no other weapon than their naked bodies; when the main road became littered with a hundred corpses in the space of twenty minutes; when the rumor that the whole city would be massacred struck terror into the populace; when ordinary civilians gathered in twos and threes to defend the bridge and the local primary school, armed with the antiquated rifles they'd found at the army reserves' training camp; when civil self-government was instated at the Provincial Office, after the authority of the central government had leaked away like an ebb tide.

While all this was going on, I was busy riding the bus in Suyuri. When I returned home and opened the front gate, I bent down to pick up the evening edition of D newspaper. Crossing the long, narrow yard, I read the lead article. GWANGJU IN STATE OF ANARCHY FOR FIFTH DAY. Blackened buildings. Trucks filled with men wearing white bandannas. The atmosphere inside the house was both subdued and unsettled. *They're not working, the phones still aren't working.* Mum kept on trying to put a call through to her family, who lived near Daein Market.

As it turned out, none of my relatives died; none were injured or even arrested. But all through that autumn in 1980, my thoughts returned to that tiny room at one end of the kitchen, where I used to lie on my stomach to do my homework, that room with the cold paper floor—had the boy used to spread out his homework on its cold paper floor, then lie stomach-down just as I had? The middle-school kid I'd heard the grown-ups whispering about. How had the seasons kept on turning for me, when time had stopped forever for him that May?

After loitering near the site of the home-fixtures store now occupying the site of my family's old house, I eventually stepped inside. The proprietor, a woman in her fifties wearing a lilac sweater, looked up from her newspaper.

"Can I help you, love?"

Having left this city when I was still young, for me its dialect was inextricably associated with my family; now that I was back, it stirred up an oddly discomfiting pathos to find perfect strangers reminding me of family members.

"There used to be a *hanok* on this spot . . . when did this building go up?" Just as I'd been thrown by the woman's dialect, so she seemed unsettled by mine, and the air of friendly camaraderie dissipated.

"You were hoping to visit the previous inhabitants?" she responded, having switched to scrupulously formal Seoul speech. I said yes; any other answer would have been too complicated. "That house was demolished the year before last." The woman's voice was completely flat. "There was an old woman living there alone; after she died her son decided there was no way he could rent out such an old house, so he had it pulled down. This current building is only temporary. We signed a lease for two years, and after that we'll leave."

I asked if she'd met the old woman's son in person.

"When we signed the contract, yes. Apparently he's a lecturer at one of the big cram schools. All the same, the pay can't be that good if he could only afford to put up a temporary building like this, could it?"

After I left the shop, I walked along the main road for some time before stopping to hail a taxi. The driver took me to this study institute that the woman had mentioned, and I flicked through the brochure until I found the staff photos. It wasn't diffi-

cult to identify the boy's older brother: a middle-aged science lecturer with thick-lensed glasses. He was wearing a brown tie with a
white shirt, and his hair was streaked with gray.

"I can maybe spare thirty minutes," he said, when we spoke on the
phone later that day, "if you come to my classroom tomorrow at
five thirty, but that's all. I hope you understand. Sometimes the
students rush their dinner so they can turn up early; in that case,
even thirty minutes might not be possible."

That night, I walk down into the subway in front of the scaffolded
Provincial Office and emerge on the other side of the street.
Pounding music spills out into the nighttime streets, neon signs
blaring as I walk against the flow of the crowd all the way to the
after-school study institute, a big one specifically for cramming
for the university entrance exams. I head to the information desk
on the ground floor. My gaze skims over the brochures displayed
there, the color leaflets advertising public lectures, the timetable
for private courses.

*I'm sorry. I thought I'd be able to finish the previous class early; in fact it
went on longer than usual.*

Please have a seat. Can I get you something to drink?

Yes, I knew the previous owner was one of Dong-ho's teachers.

I hadn't realized you would know our story.

To be honest, I was in two minds about the whole thing. At first I was worried that I didn't have anything to say, that it would be awkward to meet like this. But then I thought, what would my mother have done if she were still alive?

Well, I'll tell you: she would have agreed to meet you without a second's thought. She would have sat you down and made you listen to Dong-ho's story all the way through to the end. You wouldn't have been able to stop her if you'd tried. She lived thirty years with those words inside her. But I'm not like her, I can't dredge the past up again the way she would have.

Permission? Yes, you have my permission, but only if you do it properly. Please, write your book so that no one will ever be able to desecrate my brother's memory again.

In the small guest room near the front door, where my brother has rolled out a spare mattress and bedding for me, I spend the night tossing and turning. Every time I manage to fall asleep I find myself back in those nighttime streets, in front of the study institute. Strapping high-school boys, the kind the fifteen-year-old Dong-ho never managed to become, jostle me with their broad shoulders. *Please, write your book so that no one will ever be able to desecrate my brother's memory again.* I walk with my right hand placed over the left side of my chest, as though cradling my heart. Shadowed faces swim out of the street's dark. The face of the murdered. And of the murderer, who had thrust his dream-bayonet into my shattered chest. His blank eyes.

Whenever we had a toe war, I always won.

He was really ticklish, you see.

All I had to do was poke his foot with my big toe and he'd start squirming.

At first I couldn't tell whether he was grimacing like that because he was ticklish, or because it really hurt . . .

But then he would turn bright red and laugh.

Just as there were some soldiers who were especially cruel, so there were others who were especially nonaggressive. There were paratroopers who carried the wounded on their backs all the way to the hospital and set them down on the steps before hastening back to their posts. There were soldiers who, when the order was given to fire on the crowd, pointed the barrels of their guns up into the air so they wouldn't hit anyone. When the soldiers formed a wall in front of the corpses lined up outside the Provincial Office, blocking them from the view of the foreign news cameras, and gave a rousing chorus of an army song, there was one of their number who kept his mouth conspicuously shut.

Even the civil militia, the ones who stayed behind in the Provincial Office, displayed an attitude that wasn't dissimilar. The majority of them were willing to carry guns but, when push came to shove, couldn't actually bring themselves to fire them. When asked why they stayed behind when they knew they were staring defeat in the face, the surviving witnesses all gave the same answer: *I'm not sure. It just seemed like something we had to do.*

I'd been mistaken when I'd thought of them as victims. They'd stayed behind precisely to avoid such a fate. When I think of those ten days in the life of that city, I think of the moment when a man who'd been lynched, almost killed, found the strength to open his eyes. The moment when, spitting out fragments of teeth along with a mouthful of blood, he held his failing eyes open with his fingers so he could look his attacker straight in the face. The moment when he appeared to remember that he had a face and a voice, to recollect his own dignity, which seemed the memory of a previous life. *Break open that moment and out of it will come massacre, torture, violent repression. It gets shoved aside, beaten to a pulp, swept away in the tide of brutality. But now, if we can only keep our eyes open, if we can all hold our gazes steady, until the bitter end . . .*

Dong-ho, I need you to take my hand and guide me away from all this. Away to where the light shines through, to where the flowers bloom.

The boy with the slender neck and thin summer clothes is walking along the snow-covered path that winds between the graves, and I am following behind. The snow has already melted in the heart of the city, but here it lingers. The boy steps into a frozen drift, soaking the bottom of his tracksuit bottoms. Startled by the cold, he turns to look back at me. He smiles, and the smile reaches his eyes.

Except that, of course, there was no actual encounter among the graves. I simply wrote a note for my sleeping brother, left it on the kitchen table, and slipped out of the apartment in the early hours of the morning. Slung on my backpack, bulging with all the documents I'd gathered during my time in Gwangju, and caught the bus out of the city to the cemetery. I didn't buy flowers, didn't prepare fruit or alcohol as offerings. Coming across a box of small candles in the drawer beneath my brother's kitchen sink, I picked out three along with a lighter, but that was all.

His brother, the science lecturer, said their mother had never truly recovered after the bodies were exhumed from Mangwol-dong in 1997 and reburied in the newly constructed May 18 National Cemetery.

Like the other bereaved families, we waited until the day the fortune-teller had suggested as auspicious before we went to exhume the body. When we opened the coffins, it was every bit as gruesome as when we'd closed them. The corpse wrapped up in a plastic sheet, and a bloodstained Taegukgi covering it . . . all the same, Dong-ho's remains were in relatively good condition, because we'd been the first ones to dress the body, it hadn't been left to someone who didn't know him. So that time, too, we didn't want to entrust the job to anyone else. We unwound the cotton shroud and polished every one of his bones ourselves. I was worried that the skull would be too much for our mother, so I hurriedly picked it up myself and polished the teeth one by one. Even so, the whole experience clearly shook her to the core. I really ought to have insisted she stay at home.

Searching among the snow-covered graves, I finally found his. The Mangwol-dong gravestone, which I'd seen a long time ago, had only had his name and dates inscribed, no photo; they'd had the black-and-white photo from his school's records enlarged, and put on the new gravestone. Those flanking his all belonged to high-schoolers. I peered at those youthful faces and dark winter clothes in what were presumably middle-school graduation photos. The night before, his brother had repeatedly insisted that Dong-ho had been lucky. *Wasn't it lucky that he was shot so he died straightaway, don't you think that was lucky?* A strange fever had burned in his eyes as he begged me to agree with him. *One of the high-schoolers who was shot next to my brother at the Provincial Office, who's buried next to him now, when they exhumed him there was a hole right in the middle of his forehead, and the back of his skull was completely missing. He can't have died straightaway, so the soldiers would have shot him again to be sure that they'd finished him off.* He told me how the boy's white-haired father had wept soundlessly, his hand over his mouth.

I opened my bag and took out the three candles. I stood one in front of each boy's grave, knelt down, and lit them. I didn't pray. I didn't close my eyes, or observe a minute's silence. The candles burned steadily. Their orange flames undulating soundlessly, gradually being sucked into the center and hollowed out. Only then did I notice how incredibly cold my ankles were. Without realizing it, I'd been kneeling in a snowdrift that covered Dong-ho's grave. The snow had soaked through my socks, seeping in right through to my skin. I stared, mute, at that flame's wavering outline, fluttering like a bird's translucent wing.

ACKNOWLEDGMENTS

Of the documents which aided me during the writing of this book, I am particularly grateful to *Historical Sources on the Gwangju May Democratic Uprising* (Institute on Modern Korean History, Pale Green, 1990), *Gwangju, Women* (Gwangju Jeonnam Women's Federation, Humanitas, 2012), *We Are Righteous People* (film directed by Lee Hye-ran), *May Elegy* (film directed by Kim T'ae-il), and *5:18 Suicides—Psychological Post-mortems* (play produced by An Chu-sik). And I am deeply grateful to all of those who shared their private memories and gave me encouragement.